Dear Reader,

Happy Holidays to all of you from the staff of Silhouette Desire! Our celebration of Desire's fifteenth anniversary continues, and to kick off this holiday season, we have a wonderful new book from Dixie Browning called *Look What the Stork Brought*. Dixie, who is truly a Desire star, has written over sixty titles for Silhouette.

Next up, *The Surprise Christmas Bride* by Maureen Child. If you like stories chock-full of love and laughter, this is the book for you. And Anne Eames continues her MONTANA MALONES miniseries with *The Best Little Joeville Christmas*.

The month is completed with more Christmas treats: *A Husband in Her Stocking* by Christine Pacheco; *I Married a Prince* by Kathryn Jensen and *Santa Cowboy* by Barbara McMahon.

I hope you all enjoy your holidays, and hope that Silhouette Desire will add to the warmth of the season. So enjoy the very best in romance from Desire!

Melissa Senate

Senior Editor

Please address questions and book requests to:
Silhouette Reader Service
U.S.: 3010 Walden Ave., P.O. Box 1325, Buffalo, NY 14269
Canadian: P.O. Box 609, Fort Erie, Ont. L2A 5X3

CHRISTINE PACHECO
A HUSBAND IN HER STOCKING

SILHOUETTE *Desire*

Published by Silhouette Books

America's Publisher of Contemporary Romance

SILHOUETTE BOOKS

ISBN 0-373-76113-9

A HUSBAND IN HER STOCKING

Copyright © 1997 by Christine Pacheco

This edition published by arrangement with Harlequin Books S.A.

® and TM are trademarks of Harlequin Books S.A., used under license. Trademarks indicated with ® are registered in the United States Patent and Trademark Office, the Canadian Trade Marks Office and in other countries.

Printed in U.S.A.

Books by Christine Pacheco

Silhouette Desire

The Rogue and the Rich Girl #960
Lovers Only #1054
A Husband in Her Stocking #1113

CHRISTINE PACHECO

married her real-life hero, Jared, who proved to her that dreams really do come true. They live in Colorado with their two children, Raymond and Whitney.

Christine remembers always wanting to be a writer. She even talked her elementary school librarian into "publishing" her books. She notes that she always preferred romances because they're about that special moment when everything is possible and the future is a gift to unfold.

You can write to Christine at P.O. Box 448, Eastlake, CO 80614.

For Angie, best friend and sister.
Thanks for being my number one fan.

Also for three very special friends, and extraordinarily
talented writers, Robin Lee Hatcher, Pamela Johnson and
Lisa Craig. Thanks, guys, you're all angels!

One

Kyle Murdock swore as he turned up the collar on his black leather jacket. He raised his shoulders, fighting in vain for protection against the bite of a cold December wind.

Snow dusted his hair, and several flakes settled on his nose. Odd, only a few hours ago, the skies had been incredibly blue, hardly a cloud in sight.

Now the world was a different place. The landscape had changed. Branches had been buried beneath a blanket of white, and wind had whipped innocent flakes, plowing them into one another, making minifortresses to block his path. Kyle had been left dependent on the help of a stranger.

That was, if anyone heard his knock.

For a third time, he pounded his uncovered knuckles against unyielding wood.

Someone had to be inside the farmhouse—after all, an

inviting glow in the curtained window had attracted his attention, luring him from where the weather had stranded him. Kyle paused, listening. He heard nothing but a howl through the treetops.

The remnants of a waning Colorado sun offered no solace against the encroaching evening's threat. He shivered. The three-mile journey to the nearest town of Jefferson would be hellacious. And to be honest, Kyle wasn't sure he would even make it.

This definitely wasn't how he'd planned to spend the holiday. His sister, Pamela, and her family were expecting him. And he'd always believed Christmas was for children. There was little Kyle enjoyed more than watching his niece and nephew on Christmas morning, expressions full of belief and wonder.

Cupping his hands near his mouth, he blew air onto them and shifted his weight from leg to leg.

Slowly, accompanied by the squeak of a rusty hinge, the door to the old farmhouse opened. Light and welcoming heat spilled through the partial opening, but the soft sound of a woman's voice—soothing, yet steeled with hesitation—stole what little breath remained in his lungs.

"Can I help you?"

He moved a few inches to the right so she could see him, while she retained protection and anonymity. With a numbed thumb, he pointed toward the Harley, which was partially buried in a ditch. "My bike's stuck."

She didn't say anything, and the door denied access to her face.

"If you don't mind, I need to use your phone, maybe call a tow truck."

A few seconds of silence. Another heartbeat closer to hypothermia.

Then slowly, as if on the whisper of an angel's wings, the door opened wider.

He didn't wait for a second invitation. Wiping the soles of his boots on the step, he entered the house, transferring his wet leather gloves into one hand.

The woman sealed out the blizzard and closed Kyle in. Heat reached out, enveloping him and allowing him to suck a welcome breath deep into his chest.

He'd barely noted her eye and hair color when the noise from a sudden crash made her face drain of color.

"Excuse me," she said, turning.

Before he formed a word, she'd dashed away. Kyle stood there for a few moments, debating what to do. Mind his own business? Offer assistance?

"Darn it."

The faint sound of her pseudo curse reached him, galvanizing him into action. Not stopping to think, he followed the direction she'd taken.

As he strode through the living room, a second crash exploded. Breaking into a near run, he found her in the kitchen, kneeling in front of a huge cupboard, cans of food scattered around her.

A white dog rested a paw triumphantly on a colorful bag sporting a picture of a collie.

"Are you okay?" he asked.

Evidently startled, she swung around to look at him. A fringe of layered blond hair shaded her face, but not her wide and wary eyes.

Just then, the animal growled, hackles raised.

"Snowflake..." the woman warned, a sigh of exasperation escaping.

The mangy mutt stalked toward him, and Kyle remained rooted on the spot.

"He's more bark than bite. He wouldn't hurt a soul," she said, pushing up to a standing position.

"Hi, guy," Kyle said, holding his hand steady and not trusting her words of promise.

Snowflake growled again, then sniffed Kyle's hand.

"Mind your manners, Snowflake."

After looking toward his mistress, the dog sat. Apparently satisfied, Snowflake offered his paw. Kyle dutifully shook it.

"Some protector," she said, but rumpled Snowflake's fur affectionately when the dog returned to her side. "You managed to get all the way into the kitchen before he noticed you were in the house." Snowflake stretched out and placed his head on his paws. "Now he thinks you're his best friend."

"Obviously he senses you're in no danger."

No response.

"He's right."

The woman wiped her hand down the thigh of cream-colored leggings. For the first time he noticed just how attractive his savior was. Blond, hazel-eyed, and with ladylike curves all in the right places. A potent combination.

"Kyle Murdock," he said, extending a hand.

Surprisingly she took it. Heat met cold. He felt the icy tentacles of winter's grip melting away at her touch. Maybe, just maybe, he'd survive the storm, after all.

She was more petite than he'd realized, only a few notches above five feet. Her smaller hand disappeared inside his larger one, and he had an insane urge to hold on to it longer than was polite.

With a slight smile, she extricated her hand.

Kyle realized her wide-open eyes—expressive and large—were her most compelling feature, making a man think of long, hot nights and a bed barely big enough for two.

Right now her eyes contained a hint of caution that made the hazel color appear darker than he suspected was normal. He reminded himself he should be on his way, try to find a hotel before the storm worsened.

"Mind if I use your phone?"

She pointed to a small oak stand and said, "It's right over there."

The woman moved aside, and he took his time removing the unnecessary aviator shades from his eyes. In anonymity, he savored her subtle beauty. She wasn't gorgeous in the normal sense, but the aura of dignity and serenity she wore—a complete antithesis to what raged inside him—transcended the usual, making her seem extraordinary.

She seemed alluring, unpretentious. And so different from the woman he'd nearly married.

Dismissing the thought, as it was leading him in a direction he didn't dare go, Kyle tucked his glasses inside a pocket of his jacket. He crossed to the far wall and placed his gloves on the oak telephone stand, then thumbed through the directory until he found the single listing for a towing service. He punched in the numbers.

One ring, followed by a second. Then silence ricocheted down the line. "The phone's dead."

She swallowed deeply, folding her arms around her middle. The action stretched the cotton material of her pastel pink sweater taut across her breasts.

Kyle gulped.

He hadn't imagined the woman could have such unbelievable impact on his long neglected libido.

Turning away, he replaced the phone in its cradle, trying to erase the vivid sight of her from his mind.

Through the window above the sink, he saw the swirling snow and dreaded the thought of braving the brutal elements again. Facing her once more, he asked, "Maybe your husband could help me dig out the Harley?"

Several seconds of silence yawned between them.

"I don't have a husband."

She lived out here all alone? And opened her door to strangers? He didn't like it. Not one bit. And the fact he didn't like something that was none of his business irritated the hell out of him.

"But I do have a twelve-gauge shotgun."

He raised a brow.

"And competency in its use."

"Noted." He allowed a smile. Her tentative one was reward enough.

Just as quickly, though, the smile disappeared and her brow furrowed.

It was interesting to watch her undisguised play of emotions. She'd knotted a hand at her side, and her shoulders were slightly rounded, protective. But her whiskey-colored eyes remained wide.

"You must be cold," she said softly, almost reluctantly.

"Frozen," he admitted. "I was trying to make it to Conifer before nightfall—"

"You still can. I'll drive you. My car's in the port." Her voice held a breathless note. Obviously she was relieved to have arrived at a logical conclusion. And he hated to shatter that resolution.

She reached for a coat that hung near the back door but stopped at Kyle's words. "It's snowed in." She looked at him, and he noted a frown had settled on her features. "The carport that's at the side of the house?" he asked.

She nodded.

"I noticed when I was walking up to the door that there's two, maybe three, feet of snow blocking it."

The woman dropped her hand.

Kyle grabbed the gloves he'd placed on the phone stand and offered a wan grin. "I appreciate your help." He stuffed unwilling fingers into the soggy, cold leather, then started back toward the front door.

"Wait," she said, the word uttered so softly he wasn't sure he'd actually heard it.

Kyle Murdock stopped and leveled his disturbingly blue

eyes on her. Meghan wished for her word back. Common sense warred with what resided in her heart.

She couldn't allow a stranger who rode a Harley and wore danger cloaked by black leather to stay in her house.

Nor could she send him back out in the cold. She'd noticed the way wind had bitten at his hands and face. The elements were merciless, and her heart wouldn't permit her to turn him away.

"Yes?"

The sound of his voice worked as a balm on her lonely soul. She'd been absorbed in her work for several days. No neighbors had stopped by, and the phone hadn't rung, not even with her mother's obligatory weekly phone call. Until she had opened the front door, Meghan hadn't even realized it had been snowing.

Still, she knew not just any voice would work on her senses the way Kyle Murdock's did. No...there was something special about his. Low, deep, masculine, but with a cadence that spoke of education and reassurance, despite his attire.

She shouldn't trust him.

Was too smart to trust him.

"Mr. Murdock—"

"Kyle," he corrected her softly, sensually.

"Kyle," she repeated, the harshness of the single syllable swirling in her mind. "You appear to be stranded here."

"I'll walk to town."

"It's three miles."

"Yeah. I know."

Even though he tried to hide it, she saw his involuntary wince and noticed the way a solitary snowflake melted into the clear-night darkness of his thick hair. The leather gloves he wore were damp and stiff. And the man was already half-frozen.

If anything happened to him, Meghan would never forgive herself. That would be a greater sin than hospitality—even with the risks. Besides, she did have the gun, even if she couldn't imagine using it on him.

He didn't need to know that, though.

She swallowed, trying to moisten her mouth. "Please...stay."

"I appreciate the offer, Ms...."

He had intentionally trailed off, trying to get her to supply her name. For some reason, she steadfastly held on to that information, as if it offered protection.

"Mr. Murdock—Kyle," she amended when he opened his mouth to speak again. "There's apparently a blizzard out there. In whiteout conditions, you can't see a hundred feet in front of you. You'd be lucky not to get lost, even luckier to make it back to town."

She lowered her voice, trying to keep her tone reasonable. "Jefferson doesn't have a hotel, and Kenosha Pass is probably closed."

She swallowed, waiting for him to frame his response. Meghan forced herself to unknot the hand at her side, realizing the action had radiated tension up her arm and across her shoulder.

His response didn't matter to her. He was a grown man. If he wanted to battle the elements like the warrior he appeared to be, it was none of her concern.

At least, that's what she tried telling herself.

In honesty, she wanted him to stay.

Pretending his decision meant little or nothing to her, Meghan looked into his compelling eyes. Mouth dry as clay baked in the summer sun, she said, "You can hang your coat on the peg."

He appraised her for a few seconds, each moment seeming to grow and stretch with tension. Finally, he gave a slight nod.

Her offer had been accepted. For better or worse.

She offered a quick prayer that it was for the better.

The sound of a metal snap surrendering under his grip riveted her interest. A second snap released, then the drag of a zipper filled the kitchen.

The sound reminded her of sex.

Within seconds, he'd shucked the jacket. A crimson-colored flannel shirt snuggled against his shoulders, conforming as if made exclusively for him. The top button hung open. She wildly wondered what resided beneath.

Kyle was big, well muscled, all male. And she was stuck with him under her roof until the storm blew over. That could take twenty minutes, twenty-four hours or several days. She gulped. "I'll get you a towel," she said, desperate to get away.

Meghan went through the living room and down the hall, grabbing two towels from the linen closet. She stalled on her return, leaning against a wall. A long-denied part of her was well aware of his masculinity, along with its not-so-subtle effects on her.

Kyle Murdock bothered her.

Still, she saw that snow was steadily melting from his boots, making a mess on the worn tile flooring. Taking a deep breath, she shoved away from the wall and crossed back to the kitchen.

Kyle's large coat hung from a peg next to hers, leather contrasting with down, black contrasting with pale pink, masculine contrasting with feminine.

"Thanks," he said, reaching for a towel and scrubbing at his hair.

The result was intimately devastating.

Cropped hair now contained a hint of curl, a wayward lock falling across his forehead. Kyle shoved it back, then bent to remove his riding boots. To distract herself from the sight of him in tight, damp black jeans, she mopped water and ice with a towel.

Within a minute, he stood there, a large man in the kitchen that suddenly seemed small. "We can light a fire," she said, then wondered why her voice contained a hoarse scratch. Meghan cleared her throat and added, "To help you dry off...warm up."

He followed her into the living room. She realized no man, other than her father, had ever been in her house.

She reached for a log, only to have it slide from her grip. Meghan swore as a splinter sank into her fingertip.

Before she could extract the piece of wood, Kyle was at her side. He took her hand and stole her breath. With gentleness that belied his size, he cradled her hand in his much colder one, yet it was anything but a chill that seeped into her.

In fact, the oozing sensation that spilled through her surprised her with its welcoming warmth.

Kyle raised his palm slightly to see the sliver better, then closed the splinter between thumb and forefinger.

"Damn," he muttered, not able to grasp the small fragment well enough to pull it out. "Let me try again."

The feel of his blunted nail on her skin sent a shiver racing toward her toes.

"That hurt?"

He glanced up from what he was doing, meeting her gaze. She clearly saw his expression and read concern in the way his eyebrows drew together. "No," she whispered.

"Give me a sec, I'll get it out of there."

Kyle looked away, breaking the spellbinding hold he had over her. Meghan blinked, suddenly glad she hadn't sent him away.

"Got it."

She gasped when he pulled out the tiny piece of wood. "Okay?"

The momentary pain receded. "Thank you."

"It's the least I could do for the woman who saved me from freezing to death." He smiled then, the act transforming his features. He no longer seemed frightening or overwhelming.

Scratch that, she realized. Kyle Murdock was definitely overwhelming. Thinking he wasn't would only be pure illusion.

He released her, and the air no longer seemed as warm.

"I'll light the fire," Kyle said.

She seized the offer. "And I'll make coffee."

"That'd be great."

She headed for the kitchen.

"Ma'am?"

Meghan paused, the sound of his baritone sending skitters across her senses.

"Thank you."

She escaped.

In the kitchen again, Meghan leaned against the counter, allowing the breath she'd been holding to rush out. Her finger throbbed as she recalled the feel of him. His touch had been warm, even though it shouldn't have been—not when he was so cold.

Motions automatic, she dumped the dregs of the coffee she'd made this morning and rinsed the pot. As the caffeine-rich water gurgled into the carafe, Meghan moved to the stove, trying to block out the image of Kyle Murdock that filled her mind's eye.

She failed.

He was completely unlike her ex-husband, Jack, different from any of the men she socialized with. Kyle was rough around the edges, potent and sexy.

Not the kind of man she thought she wanted.

In an attempt to stay busy, she grabbed a spoon to stir the stew on the stove. Meghan grimaced. She'd gotten so carried away sculpting the final batch of angels that dinner had started to burn, sticking to the bottom of the pan.

Her stomach grumbled, reminding her that she'd eaten nothing all day except a bowl of cereal before the sun poked past the horizon.

Then a second, more intrusive thought rocked her: When she ate, Kyle Murdock would be sitting at the small table with her.

Her shoulders sagged. This situation was getting more and more complicated by the minute.

The faint scent of sulphur wafted on the air, and she heard the crackle of wood.

Kyle Murdock was making himself at home in her house.

The splashing noise from the coffeemaker diminished, and the bread-making machine, bought as an indulgence during a lonely Thanksgiving weekend, beeped three times, indicating it was done.

Snowflake pawed at the dog food he'd proudly pulled from the cupboard, telling Meghan in no uncertain terms that he was hungry, too.

After obligingly dumping moist food in a bowl adorned with Snowflake's name, Meghan started to stack the metal cans again, making a mental note to buy a latch for the cupboard door. Snowflake had made his favorite pastime—eating—into an annoying habit.

"Anything I can do to help?"

The sound of Kyle's rich baritone made Meghan jump. How on earth had he approached without her hearing?

She didn't look at him; instead, she picked up a metal can and added it to the pile. "Everything's under control."

"I didn't mean to scare you."

"You didn't," she lied.

He crouched next to her, muscular thigh pressed against her own, softer one. Strange sensations startled her.

Without a word, Kyle straightened the haphazard stack she'd made, then reached for the final can.

Reluctantly, she gave it to him.

He stood, offering his hand to her.

Meghan looked at him.

"I scare you."

"No." Her lie was blatant.

"I do."

She shook her head too fast.

He continued to hold out his hand. A challenge?

Against her better sense, Meghan accepted. She swore to herself she wasn't frightened, yet she was forced to admit she felt a definite awareness of him as a powerful male.

He pulled her up, not stopping until she stood barely inches from him. Her pulse thundered and heat suffused her.

She felt...womanly.

"Prove it."

She had to look up, a long way, to meet his gaze. He was tall, a little over six foot, a huge contrast to her five feet three inches. His hands were large, and as she couldn't help but notice, lacked a wedding band.

The scent of him, that of mountain air and power, combined with his proximity, his touch, his commanding hold, made Meghan moisten her teeth with her tongue. She recognized the nervous gesture, had cultivated it over the years. And she'd never hated the habit as much as she did at this second.

"Prove it," he challenged again. "Prove you're not scared of me."

She swallowed. "Prove it?"

"Give me something."

Her mind raced in symphony with the hammering of her heart.

"Your name," Kyle said softly. "Tell me your name."

Two

The challenge hung in the air between them, as powerful as the pounding of his heart. He noticed her breaths were hollow, and he saw the confusion that raced across her features.

For a second, her lashes drifted together, shutting out the honesty her eyes contained. Would she grant him the gift of her name? Could she?

Could she not?

Her lashes parted, and she looked at him. Directly. Her expression was so direct that the sensation rocked him to the soles of his feet.

"Meghan," she said.

"Meghan," he repeated, sliding the syllables around his tongue, savoring its subtle taste.

"Meghan Carroll."

He nodded. The name fit. Soft. Feminine. And with a hint of mystery. Meghan. Yeah. He liked it...liked it a lot.

She shifted; he wondered if she was waiting expectantly for his response.

"Nice name."

The release of her breath sifted through him. She had been waiting. That said a lot about her. But one thing was sure: she wasn't frightened of him. Skittish maybe, but not scared. That instantly upped his opinion of her. Kyle didn't care much for spinelessness.

"Are you hungry?" she asked.

Her tone was reluctant, as if she knew she had to ask the question, but regretted the necessity. Still, he answered with honesty. "Starving."

"I guess...you should eat with me."

"Is that an invitation?" Kyle cocked a grin.

The tension on her face lessened. "Sorry, I didn't mean for it to sound that way."

"What way?" He waited for her to respond, wondered if she'd do it with the same frankness she'd shown so far.

"Rude. That was rude, and I'm not usually rude."

"Do you usually have strange men in your kitchen?"

With her right hand, she brushed errant strands of hair away from her face. He stood close to her, closer than she probably liked, yet he didn't back off.

Kyle caught the faint whiff of her understated perfume—light with a hint of unfulfilled promise—and couldn't recall the last time he'd been with a woman as sensually appealing as Meghan.

He wondered why he suddenly felt hungry, not physically but emotionally.

"No," she finally admitted. "You're the first man who's been in my kitchen."

The information stunned him, pleased him. It shouldn't have, but it did. And how.

"I'll serve," Meghan said, shattering the tension that had slowly been building. "If you set the table."

"Ah, a modern woman."

She gave a small smile that transformed her features and made his insides flame with awareness.

"You can do the dishes, too," she said.

"Do I smell homemade bread?"

She indicated a small white appliance. "Bread-maker—my one extravagance this year."

"All this for the measly price of setting the table and washing the dishes?"

"I hate doing dishes."

Slowly, she'd revealed several aspects of her personality. Kyle wanted each stripped and laid bare before him. And he had a few thoughts about what to do once they were. "Lady, you've got a deal."

Kyle hadn't been in a kitchen like this for years. It covered at least three hundred square feet, huge, rambling and, by today's standards, a waste of space.

But he remembered a similar kitchen, always filled with the scent of spice. Kyle also recalled helping his grandmother, Grandma Aggie, in that kitchen, begging for the honor of cracking the eggs against the ancient metal strip surrounding the counter.

"Something funny?" Meghan asked.

Startled at her perception, he looked up from setting bowls and silverware on the table.

"You're smiling," she added.

"My grandmother had a kitchen like this. Brings back memories." His own designer kitchenette didn't look anything similar to either. Meghan's kitchen didn't have a microwave; his was built in above the stove he'd never used. Nor did she have a dishwasher. But she had something he didn't: a feeling of home.

Kyle realized he wouldn't have been as comfortable in her home if her kitchen had resembled his. That thought gave him pause, made him question, again, his reasons for deciding to return to Chicago and accept control of Murdock Enterprises—his father's business—in the New Year.

Snowflake entered the kitchen, toenails clicking on the worn floor. He curled beneath the table, apparently anxious for handouts. Judging by the extra few pounds on the mutt, Meghan was an indulgent mistress.

A soft heart.

No surprise there. He wouldn't be shocked to learn Snowflake had shown up on her doorstep—much like Kyle—and that she'd kept the animal.

Meghan poured two cups of coffee, then joined Kyle at the table. Their knees brushed. Their glances collided. And then she slammed him in the solar plexus by licking her lower lip.

Longing. And an urge to possess.

Neither feeling was welcome. But there they were, raw and honest. Trouble was, there wasn't a thing he could do about them.

Kyle had promised she was in no danger from him. In that instant, he wondered if he'd lied.

He wanted Meghan Carroll with an intensity that stunned him.

And he wouldn't—couldn't—have her.

He was merely passing through town, not intending to stay. His life lay elsewhere, much as he hated that fact. So far his search for answers had revealed only one thing—you were who you were.

No escape.

Exerting the iron control for which he was famous, he tamped down the flare of wanting and picked up the ladle.

"Don't scoop any from the bottom."

He paused.

"The bottom part is burned." She gave a little shrug. "I got carried away with my work. Forgot about dinner."

Judging by her size, she forgot often. She needed a keeper, Kyle realized. But he couldn't fill that role.

He envied the man who would.

Taking stew from the pan, he filled her bowl, then his.

She met his eyes, and for a few seconds, silence shrouded the empty house. Did she feel it, too, this tug that was as undeniable as it was real?

And what the hell were they supposed to do?

She raised a spoon to her lips and sipped. Kyle's gut tightened. Desperate to distract himself, he followed suit. He allowed that first bite to linger, enjoying the flavor. Realizing he was close to a sigh, he swallowed. "My grandmother used to make stew like this."

Wistful sadness dropped her tone. "I never knew my grandmother."

"I'm sorry," he said sincerely. His grandmother had been the single bright spot in a bleak childhood. He didn't remember his mother—he was too young when she died. His father had thrown himself into building the business Kyle's grandfather had started. Precious little time had been left over for either Kyle or his older sister, Pamela.

Yet Grandma Aggie had tried to fill all the voids. She'd given them birthdays and holidays, given them love and hope.

Meghan broke off a piece of her bread, then fed it to a vigilant Snowflake.

Kyle had a sudden insight into his own lonely life-style. No one cared if he came home at night. No one noticed.

It didn't matter. Never had. Maybe never would.

Ruthlessly shoving aside the sober feelings, Kyle said, "This is a fabulous farmhouse." His skilled eye had noted the solid construction, along with the repairs the house cried out for.

Yet there was something else... He drummed his fingers on the table. Something bothered him about the farmhouse, as if it were lacking a detail just beyond the obvious. Try as he might, Kyle couldn't put his finger on the missing element.

"I fell in love with the house the first time I saw it."

"How long have you been here?"

She set down her spoon. He'd done it again, pushed past the impersonal to the personal. He stopped his motions and waited for her response. When he'd given up, convinced she'd change the subject, she said, "Three years."

"You've lived out here all alone for three years?"

"Well, not alone, I have Snowflake—"

"And a shotgun," he added.

That brought a slight smile. He relished the victory. "Do you ever get lonely, Meghan?"

"I enjoy my own company," she hedged.

Why did it matter to him, anyway? In less than a day, he would climb on the back of the Beast and continue home to Chicago. Meghan would be a comfortable memory, one that would fade once the routine set back in.

A lie.

He'd told himself a lie. Meghan Carroll wasn't a woman easily forgotten.

After dinner, while she straightened up, he washed the dishes, as promised. Suds foamed everywhere, since he didn't have a clue how long he should have squirted the liquid under the running water. To her credit, she didn't say a word.

"Shall we finish our coffee in the living room?" she offered.

Grateful for an excuse to exit the kitchen before she assigned him another task he wasn't up to, he agreed. While he attempted to wash the white bubbles down the drain, she topped their coffee.

He thought he caught a mischievous glint in her eyes

but, since she didn't say anything, dismissed it as a trick of the lighting.

Snowflake curled up on a rug, and Meghan took the high-backed chair near the crackling fireplace. Kyle tossed another piece of wood on the fire, poked at the still-burning log, then closed the safety grate.

He stood, looking at the blowing snow through the ice-encrusted window. Wind whipped flakes against the pane, making him shiver. Yet a cozy fire licked at dried timber. Outside was frightful, but inside, was so...

That's when he realized it.

What was missing.

Christmas.

No sign of Christmas—not a single one—existed anywhere in the old farmhouse.

By this time of year, only four days before Christmas, his grandmother would have pestered Granddad into cutting a tree. Evergreen arrangements would adorn each end table, and garlands would hang from every possible place.

Pinecones would dangle from the mantel, tied together with red velvet. Presents, wrapped in every color imaginable, would have been artfully placed beneath the tree's bottom branches, at least two packages bearing tags lettered with Kyle's name.

Even though Grandma Aggie had passed away, Christmas still meant a lot to him. It meant a chance to be with Pam, Mark and their kids, and its absence here felt completely wrong.

Tucking a hand in a front pocket of his jeans, he turned back to face her. "Meghan?"

She looked at him over the rim of the coffee cup, steam rising to bathe her face. Although she didn't say anything, hazel eyes questioned him.

"You don't have a Christmas tree."

The fireplace crackled. Snowflake lifted a paw and placed it across his head.

Softly, she said, "I don't see the point anymore."

"Don't see...?"

She raised her shoulders defensively. "I live out here alone."

Even his empty apartment had an artificial tree, which the housekeeper had dragged from a box after Thanksgiving. "So?"

"Christmas is just another day."

"Is it?" he asked. "What about the meaning of Christmas—family, caring, sharing?"

"What about it, Kyle?" She placed her coffee cup on a coaster on the end table and looked up at him. "What makes Christmas so special? It isn't for me."

She blinked, as if she was trying to disguise some emotion. "I get up, have my coffee, take care of my chores, try to call my parents—the lines are usually all busy—then get to work. It's another day."

He heard a shallow, underlying pain, maybe tinged with regret. What was it about him—about her—that made him want to take that hurt and erase it, replacing it with something new, with warm memories?

Kyle dismissed the thought; it was as unwelcome as it was impossible.

He wouldn't be here long enough. Besides, what right did he have to insist she celebrate Christmas? It was a personal choice.

But damn it, that foolish, sentimental urge just refused to be tamped down. The house all but cried out for attention, for warmth and spontaneity, for a family.

Too bad, he told himself ruthlessly. She wanted no part of it.

The lamps flickered threateningly. Wind howled through the windows, rattling the glass. The fire hissed and jumped.

"Do you have flashlights? Maybe some candles?" If he didn't miss his guess, the electricity would soon fail.

"In the kitchen." She stood, seemingly anxious to be alone.

He made no move to follow her. Obviously he bothered her, probably more than she cared to admit. Truth to tell, she bothered him. More than *he* cared to admit.

The lights blinked again, driving him into action. It promised to be a long night. "Meghan?" he asked, following her into the kitchen. "Where's your wood storage?"

"There's a closet right there."

While she gathered a flashlight and candles, he grabbed two kerosene lanterns from a shelf. In the living room, she placed everything on the coffee table, working around the oblivious Snowflake.

By the time he stacked the second load of wood next to the fireplace, the lights gave a final flicker.

Kyle and Meghan's eyes met. Then their world faded to complete darkness.

Intimacy seemed to take on a life of its own. Kyle was very much aware of the woman standing near him.

"Kyle?"

"Right here. I'll have a lantern lit in a sec." The absence of light enhanced his other senses, making the sound of her voice more provocative. He noticed the soft ebb and flow of her breaths, the very feminine scent of her potent perfume and the indescribable impact of her presence.

Want flared in timing with the match he struck against a brick. Within moments, the whiff of kerosene hung pungently in the air. Mother Nature blasted the house and tension dropped over them.

"I guess you're well and truly stuck now," she said.

He nodded, then noticed the way dim lantern light and fire glow played on her blond hair.

Temptation.

Kyle tried to resist, told himself to resist, ordered himself to resist.

And failed.

He reached out to her, traced his fingertip down her cheek—soft, so soft. Caught in the spell of lantern light and snow, she seemed ethereal, a result of the magical season.

She stiffened but didn't pull away.

Their gazes locked, he read loneliness in her eyes and knew it matched his own.

Snowflake belatedly barked, shattering the sensual moment. Meghan slowly moved away, then lit a second lantern. She adjusted the wick when black smoke filled the glass carafe.

He couldn't help but notice the way her hand shook.

"I'll...er, set up one of the bedrooms for you."

"The couch is fine," he said. "Don't go to any trouble."

"It's no trouble," she assured him, but she was grateful for his suggestion. The farther away he was the better.

"I don't mind the couch."

She nodded and disappeared for a few minutes, carrying a flashlight, a lazy Snowflake her reluctant companion. Kyle sat on the couch and drank from his coffee in silence. Now that he'd spent an evening with someone special in a Colorado Christmas storm, it made him realize how empty and bleak his own life was.

Even if the snow disappeared overnight and he made it home for the holidays, he would still face January 2 as a lonely man.

Although Meghan might not celebrate Christmas, she knew the meaning of the season. She'd taken in a perfect stranger, given him food, warmth, shelter. If that wasn't the spirit of Christmas, he didn't know what was.

A tinder leaped, hitting the grate.

Kyle vowed to find a way to pay Meghan back for the generous gift of her hospitality.

She returned carrying blankets and sheets, even a feather pillow. The linens smelled fresh, as if dried in a breeze—not in an appliance.

While Meghan plumped the pillow, he wondered what her hair would look like spread across the soft surface.

Kyle stood and reached for the sheet she'd draped over the chair. "I'll do that," he said, freezing her midmotion.

After a few seconds, she said, "Thanks, but I've got it." Meghan accepted the sheet from him, her fingers rubbing across his. Her eyes opened wide before she blinked and turned away.

Motions smooth and economical, she tucked the sheet between the cushions and couch back. Her cotton sweater moved with her, riding high and affording him a view of her thighs and hips.

It was going to be a hell of a long night, he realized again—and not just because of the cold.

He shook out a blanket, then spread it on top of the sheet. If he didn't do something—anything—he would succumb to the impulse of touching her again, bothering her even more than he already had. That would be unpardonable, a breach of her hospitality.

The resolution didn't stop him from remembering the feel of her, though.

She turned back to face him, picked up a lantern. The light shed a halo of gold around her, caressing her features the way he wanted to.

"Is there anything else I can do for you?"

Even in the limited lighting, he noticed her blush. The question had been unintentionally intimate; he let it go. Instead, he shook his head.

"In that case, good night."

He waited until she reached the bottom of the stairs, then spoke. "Meghan?"

She paused.

"I'll..."

"Yes?"

"Find a way to make this up to you."

"That's not necessary."

Which was why he was doubly determined to repay her. Meghan started up the stairs, leaving him alone and feeling more lonely than he had in years.

Meghan tossed and turned.

Muted sounds from the living room filtered up the stairs. She heard her houseguest moving around.

Undressing?

She thumped her pillow.

The night chill seemed to seep beneath her blankets, freezing her. Her toes curled against the cold.

She ordered herself to go to sleep. The moment her eyes closed, though, thoughts of Kyle made her imagination leap with possibilities. Vivid pictures painted on top of what she'd already noted: broad shoulders, lean hips, muscular thighs.

In her mind, she saw his naked torso, his back, his biceps.

She cracked open her eyes and automatically searched for the digital display telling the time. Remembering the electrical failure, she turned over, willing herself to relax.

The second attempt was no more successful than the first.

She still couldn't believe she'd invited the man to spend the night, couldn't believe the way he'd taken over and performed several tasks, lightening the load of her responsibilities.

And she especially couldn't believe the way her body reacted to his, seeming to hum with vibrant awareness.

His touch hadn't been anything, really—less than a good-night kiss on a first date. But her insides had turned molten...a crackling need sparked to life. The feel of his finger on her cheek had made her want more, want to turn her head into his palm and rest it there.

He hadn't meant anything, but heaven help her, she'd wanted more.

She groaned. Meghan Carroll did not respond this way to just any man.

It'd been a long time since Jack—years since her heart had raced. Yet Kyle had done that—oh, so effectively—in mere moments.

He hadn't respected the lines she'd drawn around her personal life, either. Kyle had tried to push past her walls, asking for answers she had never given anyone. She shivered, this time not because of the cold but because she suspected Kyle would demand more if he stayed.

She hoped she was strong enough to brave the storm that was Kyle Murdock.

For several hours, she dozed off and on. A vicious blast of wind rattled the house, shaking the window. Snowflake whimpered and bounded onto the bed, startling Meghan from her disturbed sleep.

She was shivering, the temperature in the bedroom having fallen sharply. No matter how tight a ball she curled into, she couldn't produce any heat.

Conceding the battle, she sat up and fumbled with the flashlight. After reaching for her heavy terry cloth robe, Meghan climbed from the bed, sliding her feet into furry slippers.

She tiptoed down the stairs, intending to make a cup of tea to warm her up before trying to sleep again.

One hand gripping the banister, she paused, the glow from the flashlight falling on Kyle. Six foot plus of raw masculine energy was sprawled across the cushions of her too-small couch. Suddenly, breathing became an act requiring concentration.

A blanket covered him from the waist down, but his

chest was bare and every bit as well developed as her imagination teased.

Even in sleep, he didn't look innocent, not at all. In fact, he still appeared darkly dangerous.

She swallowed. Aware of acting like a voyeur, she consciously averted her gaze and directed the beam of light at the floor as she continued past him, Snowflake on her heels.

In the kitchen, she lit a lantern, filling the room with a soft glow, and momentarily banishing the blizzard's fury.

As she turned on the tap and filled the kettle, Meghan released a breath she hadn't realized she was holding. Glad, for once, of the ancient gas stove that didn't need electricity, she found matches and lit the burner.

In the silence of the storm, Meghan reached for the clay angel sitting on the counter and traced her fingers across the wings she'd painstakingly sculpted.

This angel, Lexie, was her favorite, named after the grandmother who'd died before she was born. It was one of Meghan's first-ever attempts at sculpting, yet the one angel she'd been unable to part with. "Well, Lexie, what are we going to do?"

Lexie maintained her perpetually serene smile, offering Meghan some comfort. She replaced the figurine. As the kettle began to hiss, she switched off the gas.

Snowflake plopped down near his bowl, and Meghan carried her cup and tea bag to the table and stirred in a single spoon of sugar.

"Is there tea for two?"

Her spoon clattered to the table. She looked up.

Kyle lazed against the doorjamb, wearing an unbuttoned shirt, tight jeans...and a tempting-as-sin smile.

And the problem was, Meghan realized as her insides constricted into a hyper-aware knot, she was tempted.

Heaven help her, she was tempted.

Three

"Do you see them?" The newer angel's words were breathless, woven on puffs of air coming from a divinely distant realm.

Lexie smiled as another blip of pure-pink energy zapped past her. "It's a good sign," the older angel agreed, folding in her right wing gracefully when another burst of sensually radiant energy sailed by.

"I'm so glad we were able to squeeze so much snow from the clouds." Grandma Aggie's eyes opened wide and she looked over her shoulder, as if fearing repercussions from the admission. She twisted her hands together, then she sighed. "Oh, Lexie, do you suppose our reprimand will be terrible?"

Lexie smiled serenely, no stranger to breaking the rules. Where Meghan was concerned, Lexie often followed her heart rather than her head. She simply couldn't bear to watch her darling granddaughter suffer. And now with a co-conspirator…well, Archangel Michael had said it best, himself…trouble had doubled since Aggie's arrival several years ago, when the two had become fast celestial friends. It hadn't been long before their individual goals for Meghan and Kyle had become a mutual plan. "I'm sure we'll have some answering to do."

Another strand of Grandma Aggie's hair, black as the coal Santa would leave for some, turned gray.

"But it's Christmas, and the others are distracted making wishes come true," Lexie added. "And that's all we're doing. Trying to make wishes come true."

"But neither of them wished for each other."

"That's simply beside the point," Lexie said, sending a mental message of peace to her partner in crime—or in this case, romance.

"They'll realize soon enough they wished for each other," Lexie continued, then added her silent hope that her promise would prove true. "If we're very lucky, Meghan will believe in Christmas again. Then we'll be rewarded with wings of gold, instead of being chastised." She straightened the halo that had, oddly enough, tipped to one side.

"Oh, dear me, do look!" Aggie pointed to Meghan.

A flush had stolen over Meghan's face, and her breathing pattern had changed, becoming more shallow by the moment.

Kyle, Aggie's grandson, took a step into the kitchen.

"He is handsome," Lexie approved, holding her hands near her heart and feeling the soothing balm of heat.

"Not only that, but he's a good person inside," Aggie added loyally.

The sensual chemistry between the two humans wavered in the air, sending shock waves of vibrancy into the atmosphere.

Kyle's jeans rode low on his hips as he took another step, skittering tension everywhere.

"My...my goodness," Aggie breathed.

"I guess the rest is up to them." Lexie spread her wings wide, enveloping the newer arrival in the protective folds. "Er...it's not polite to peek when things like this start to..." She searched for the right word, cleared her throat. "Percolate."

"Oh. Oh, my."

Lexie cracked her gum, ignoring the gentle waves of chastisement buffeting her from above. "Now to think of a suitable excuse so our silver wings don't get taken away. Puppy duty is entirely too much work...."

Kyle took a second, then third, and finally a fourth step into the kitchen, and Meghan slumped in her chair.

There was something about him, something so real and powerful that made rational thought impossible.

She picked up her cup, holding it with a shaky hand, well aware of Kyle's intense perusal. Fingers slightly unsteady, she raised her tea to take a deep drink, only to succeed in scalding her tongue.

Kyle took a seat across from her. The sight of his half-naked body was a visual feast. His chest seemed broader this close, and her mind noted each detail of his muscular build. Well-developed biceps spoke of strength, making her wonder what it might feel like to be cradled, protected.

The scattering of dark hair made her fingers tingle in anticipation. The way denim conformed to his muscles induced thoughts she hadn't known she was capable of.

Meghan hadn't ever had a lewd thought.

Until now.

Even though the power had failed, electricity all but hummed around them.

He reached for the teakettle and grabbed a mug from the

cup tree on the table. His hand stilled, and he glanced around. "Did you hear something?"

Meghan heard precious little above the rush of blood humming through her veins.

"A rustling, like feathers?"

She shook her head.

With a shrug, he said, "Must be hearing things." Then he placed the mug on the table. "How do you do this?"

"Do what?" The words emerged weak and broken. Breathing took an act of incredible concentration.

"Make tea." He grinned. "I haven't done it before."

Her breath expelled in a heartbeat.

"Which do I put in first, the water or the bag?"

She'd never imagined that mundane conversation could require so much effort. Then again, this was a first for her. "Tea bag first."

"Gotcha."

He followed her instructions, then started to squeeze the excess tea from the bag.

"Don't." She automatically reached across the table to stop his motion, placing her hand on top of his.

He dropped the tea bag.

The warmth of human touch stole into her.

She gulped, commanding her brain to move her hand away.

She couldn't.

Then Kyle sealed her hand within his. And suddenly, all oxygen vanished from the room.

Her skin was warm and soothed, her heart fast and furious. Her mouth was dry while her insides moistened with recognized need.

She shook her head, trying to dispel the unwelcome feeling. She didn't want, didn't need anyone. Especially Kyle Murdock.

But their gazes locked, and urgency in his eyes communicated to her.

Imminent danger cloaked her, and she needed to escape. With more resolution than she actually felt, she pulled her hand free.

She blinked, telling herself she'd imagined the sensory assault.

But her hand trembled.

She hadn't imagined it. It was there, and real as anything she'd ever experienced. Looking skyward, she offered a silent plea for help. Her emotions were tangled around and within her physical response, and she didn't know what to do, how to act. The snow needed to end—now. The roads needed to be clear by dawn.

A gust of wind slashed the window with a sheet of driven white snow.

Obviously, she would receive no help from above.

Which left her alone…with Kyle and simmering awareness.

"Does it really make a difference?"

She stalled for seconds, then gave in and looked at him. "Make a difference?" Meghan tried for a light, airy tone. She'd been so caught up in mental, as well as the all-too physical, images of him, she hadn't been able follow his conversation.

He grinned, cocking his head to the side. Coherent thought was impossible when that damnable lock of hair fell across his forehead again. She wanted to brush back the wayward hair, absorb each tactile sensation.

"The tea, not squeezing it?"

A thousand sensations had crowded her; not a single one of them concerned tea. "It's, er, less bitter that way."

"Some things are less bitter if they do get squeezed."

Oh, Lord. She was sinking. Drowning.

This was all so unreal, couldn't possibly be happening.

Winter's fury made her feel isolated and stranded, as if Kyle were the only link to the outside world.

After a few more moments of intense study, Kyle seemed to sense her discomfort. Breaking eye contact, he put two spoons of sugar in his cup, stirred, sipped, then cringed.

"It's not coffee," she supplied, retreating from intimacy like a shadow hiding from the sun.

"You can say that again." He added another mound of sugar, then stirred again.

"Next time I'll make instant coffee."

"This is fine."

His lie hung on the air, making her smile. Kyle was a lousy liar—maybe on a par with her.

"Okay, so I'll choke it down."

She thought of seizing the opportunity to vanish back upstairs. For a reason she was reluctant to name, she suppressed the nudge of self-preservation and stayed.

Meghan hadn't known she liked to flirt with danger...until Kyle showed up on her doorstep.

Now it seemed she not only wanted to skirt it, but wanted to experience, feel, see, taste it. She wondered if he'd be as apt a teacher as she pictured.

With unabashed interest, she watched him swallow another drink of tea, cataloging his frown. "There's hot chocolate in the cupboard," she said.

With eagerness, he stood and asked, "Which cupboard?"

She pointed, and he opened the door, choosing the box with miniature marshmallows and real sugar. Then he picked up Lexie, her clay angel, from the counter and carried both back to the table.

Lantern light danced as the air stirred, creating a secluded atmosphere. Maybe, she told herself as he invaded her space again, knees brushing beneath the table, she should have run while she had the chance.

"My Grandmother Agnes, or Grandma Aggie as I called her, used to collect angels," Kyle said, taking another mug from the tree. This time, after his first taste, he gave a satisfied nod. He picked up the molded piece of clay with rosy cheeks and a somewhat battered halo.

It seemed ridiculously small in his big hands, yet he securely cradled the miniature in his palm. Safe. That's how Lexie looked. And how Meghan felt, despite the myriad reasons she should feel anything but.

"Used to?" she asked softly.

"She died a few years ago."

Meghan heard the undisguised layer of pain in his tone. "I'm sorry."

"I am, too. She was someone very special." He slid the angel onto the tabletop, his fingertip resting briefly on the dried flowers Lexie clutched. "Do you remember where you bought it? I'd love to get one to remember her."

"I made it. She's modeled after my grandmother, Lexie."

"Impressive."

His note of approval brought a flush of pleasure to her face.

He leaned back in his chair. Kyle either didn't notice or chose to ignore his very real impact on her.

"Is it a hobby or a job?" he asked.

"I sell them to local stores."

"You make them here?"

"I have a studio upstairs."

He nodded. "I'd like to see it."

Her mind momentarily blanked. No one, ever, had seen her studio. It was her sanctuary, her escape. She didn't allow trespassers. "Sure," she lied. Then she sought refuge behind the knowledge he wouldn't be here long enough to ask again.

"Do you have any more for sale? Angels, that is."

"Plenty." She cringed, thinking of the extra inventory adorning the shelves in her studio. "I finished up a batch when you got here. I was supposed to deliver them to town this evening."

"Maybe I could take some off your hands."

Polite. The man was polite. Manners of a saint. The sex appeal of a sinner.

"Is business good year-round, or does it peak at Christmas?"

There was that word again, *Christmas*. She distrusted the word and his motives as much as if he'd just waved a sprig of mistletoe over her head.

Mistletoe.

Just the thought of standing with him, beneath mistletoe made her imagine the feel of his lips on hers.

She banished the very real, very unsettling image—or tried to.

"Meghan?"

"Christmas is the best, businesswise, but I'm working toward building distribution throughout the state. I hope that will make things less seasonal."

"Why do you dislike it so much?"

She blinked. "Dislike what?"

"Christmas." He laid the word between them. He met her gaze, captured it, compelled her to continue looking at him. "You wince every time I mention it."

"I don't," she protested, cursing his powers of observation. No other person had so skillfully cut through her outer layer of defense and gone for the heart. She wrapped her hands around the cup of tea, trying to ward off the sudden chill.

"You do."

Although Kyle appeared outwardly relaxed, she instinctively recognized the deception. His brows were drawn together in intense scrutiny, and his gaze never wavered from being fixed on her.

"You just did it again," he stated flatly. "Flinched."

She wondered what he did for a living, but knew whatever it was, he did it well. Single-minded determination was evident in his falsely relaxed posture, tone and questions. He might allow a brief respite, but he always returned to his point.

Meghan shuddered as she toyed with the image of what it might be like to be pursued by him with that awesome, single-minded determination.

He didn't speak, apparently satisfied to wait on her response.

Kyle took a drink, then returned the mug to the table soundlessly—at least she assumed it to be soundlessly, since her thumping heart filled her ears. He wouldn't waver. And unless she wanted him to return to the conversation over and over, she had to tell him, sharing the painful memories she'd tried to bury. Maybe if she told him, he'd leave her alone. "I don't dislike Christmas itself."

"Go on."

"It's the associations with Christmas that I can do without."

He fingered Lexie's fragile halo, which was made from dried flowers. Wind lashed the window with a howl, as if violently disagreeing with Meghan's assessment of the holiday. She shuddered. Yet in the anonymity of the barely luminated night, she found courage. Even though her voice hardly cracked a decibel above a whisper, she confessed, "I've never had a real Christmas."

Kyle's brows arched. "Never had...?"

"My mother and father are..." She battled disloyalty, hating to say anything bad about anyone—particularly her parents. She settled for a half truth. "Absorbed in their own lives."

Meghan swept the thick layers of hair back from her face, holding her hand on top of her head while memories dragged to the surface on stubborn heels. "I had nannies who resented not having time off to spend with their own families."

"Just what kind of parents do you have?"

"Rich ones."

She saw him take in the kitchen, with its faded vinyl, outdated appliances and seen-better-days curtains. Despite her best intentions, she gave a shallow smile. "I don't accept their money. They send a check every year." She waited a couple of beats, then added, "At—"

"Christmas." This time, Kyle winced.

She dropped her hand and raised her shoulder in a short shrug. "I send it to the childrens' shelter."

"They don't spend the holiday with you?" he asked incredulously.

"Aspen's quite a drive from here."

"So they live in the state?"

She shook her head. "They have places in France and Florida. They just fly to Colorado for two weeks each year. Great skiing. Even better parties."

"And they don't come to see you?"

"They did. *Once.*"

Kyle's four-letter word was ferocious and forceful. She grimaced. "And Santa Claus?" he asked, leaning forward, adding to the intimacy, stealing rational thought.

"Didn't have time to stop at my house."

"Jeez, Meghan, what the hell kind of life is that for a kid?"

"At least it was a little better than the Christmases when I was left at boarding school."

Kyle's hands tightened into fists. "That's not the way it is." Each word was tight, leashed with control. "Not the way it should be."

"Maybe not," she said softly, the sharpness of his voice reverberating in the quiet. "But it's the only way I've ever known. There was one night," she said softly, "that my nanny found me asleep on the stairs, waiting for Santa Claus, for my parents to come home and tell me they loved me, waiting for some of the Christmas magic people talk about."

In a painful whisper, she added, "It never happened."

"I'm going to change that," he vowed.

For the hesitant flash of a stolen moment in time, she believed him.

Reality rushed back in an unwelcome return. She hadn't felt disappointment only once. She'd experienced the sting twice, as if the heavens weren't satisfied with a single serving.

A mother's inflicted pain had been nothing in comparison to the anguish caused by a man who'd stood in front of a preacher, looked in her eyes and swore he would love and cherish her, forever.

And that part was her secret.

Years later, Meghan still had trouble believing anyone could be as coldly merciless as Jack had been on their first holiday together.

Feeling a tear form, she rapidly blinked, refusing to give in again.

"You don't believe me."

Meghan might be a fool once, maybe even twice, but never three times. She met Kyle's eyes, as bleak as his words. "No. I don't. Christmas isn't for everyone. It isn't for me."

In a fluid motion that belied his size, he stood, the chair toppling with a resounding crash. He demolished the distance between them, placing his hands on her shoulders and pulling her up to face him.

She tried to swallow, but there wasn't enough moisture

to make it possible. His masculine scent surrounded her, making her thinking clash simultaneously into thoughts of safety and danger. She feared for her own sanity and her ability to keep a foothold on the reality life had dealt her.

His look was purposeful.

Meghan trembled with anticipation.

When he drew her closer with firm pressure, she didn't resist. Just for now she wanted to succumb to the thundering impulses inside.

She felt his hands in her hair, tangling in the sleep-tousled strands. Gently, he moved a hand down, skimming her neck, her spine, spreading across her upper back and holding her tight.

His chest filled her vision, and she wildly wondered if that V of hair dipping below his waistband would lead to...

Kyle eased her closer, closer. His shirt parted. She rested her cheek against his chest, matted with dark hair. Beneath her ear, his heart thudded reassuringly.

Feelings, sensations, stole through her.

Warmth.

Hunger.

Promise.

And want.

Oh, Lord, the *want* was the worst.

"Meghan?"

She looked everywhere, anywhere, but up at him. "Hmm?"

"Look at me."

She battled urge, and fought her strong reluctance at the same time. Meghan didn't do...this. She didn't allow a man into her house, didn't allow a man to take her in his arms.

Maybe there was something to this Christmas business, Meghan thought. There had to be. Why else would she behave so irrationally by welcoming him into her house, her life?

"Look at me," he repeated.

Meghan moved away from the comfort of his chest.

"I'm going to take away the hurt. That's a promise you can take to the bank."

"You actually think you mean that."

"I do mean it, Meghan. I'll make you believe, too."

"You'll be gone as soon as the snow stops."

He released her gaze, then placed a palm protectively alongside her face. "Not until I show you Christmas."

She searched his face for meaning, for understanding. "Why? Why should it matter to you?"

He offered a small shrug. "Maybe because everyone deserves a Christmas to remember."

And that was all the more reason for her not to believe.

Kyle pulled her close again, back into his protective embrace. How long they stayed like that, she didn't know. It was a hug, she told herself, nothing more. Earlier today, she'd been wary of a stranger entering her house, now she was entrusting her body.

But not her heart. Not ever again her heart.

"We've got a problem, Meghan."

From where she rested, his voice was muffled.

"The cold. It's my guess your room is colder than downstairs."

Right now, cold was the furthest thing from her mind. The shiver sliding down her spine had little to do with the lack of heat.

"I won't be able to sleep knowing you're upstairs freezing."

Gusting snow was whipped to a howling frenzy. Glass panes jittered in their casings. A candle jumped, settling to an uneasy flicker.

Kyle drew a breath and said, "We need to be smart about this."

She shuddered as his implications seeped in along with the frigid temperature.

"Body heat is one of the best ways to keep warm."

She moistened her lower lip, and the damp only seemed to chill her more. "What did you have in mind?"

He looked at her, danger and a banded desire smoldering in the depths of his eyes.

"We need to sleep together."

Four

"**I**'ll be a perfect gentleman.... Promise."

Meghan gulped.

She didn't believe him.

Didn't trust him.

The idea was ludicrous. Insane. She couldn't sleep with him, despite his promise.

He stood there, not making any move toward her, not trying to influence her decision.

Meghan prided herself on her take-charge approach to life. So why did one man possess the ability to completely knock her off-kilter?

The thought of being so near him made her insides contort into a painfully pleasurable knot. Logic said Kyle's suggestion was rational. Instinct argued it was anything but.

She rubbed her arms, noticing the goose bumps below the thickness of terry cloth. The house temperature had slipped several more degrees. She just wished it hadn't take her resolve along with it.

"Made a decision?"

"You're right," she said, hoping her voice hadn't emerged as wobbly as it sounded to her ears.

"So you'll sleep with me?"

Color seeped from her face.

"Sleep," he repeated softly.

Was it only her imagination that had placed a sensual spin on the word? "I didn't think you meant anything else," she said, nearly choking on the fib.

He nodded.

She led the way to the living room, her legs feeling as though they'd been weighted with lead. "We'll need more bedding," she said, turning and bumping into him.

Her heart's tempo increased.

From the danger?

Or from the recognition of awareness?

Catching her around the shoulders, he steadied her with those large, capable hands.

"I'll be right back." She hurried away.

Directing the flashlight's shallow beam at the floor, Meghan took the stairs at a near jog. Over and over, she questioned her decision to spend the night beneath the same blanket as Kyle Murdock.

The man was a stranger.

And saw himself as a savior.

Upstairs, she grabbed an extra pillow and comforter from the closet. Clutching them to her chest like a shield, she thought of the gleam she'd noticed in his eye.

Danger.

She was smarter than to succumb to the powerful allure. She'd been hurt before, knew the lasting ramifications of unbearable ache. Still, a wayward, never before tapped part of her yearned to reach out and grab that which she had never experienced.

She tamped down the unholy urge.

In the heart, hurt lasted longer than fleeting pleasure.

And yet, as frigid air crept up the inside of her robe, she trembled. Her shoulders hunched as she sought to preserve her remaining heat. She was resolved. She didn't want to stay awake all night, teeth chattering.

Better to face the danger Kyle posed than the danger of freezing.

Closing the closet door with her hip, she slowly descended the stairs, finding him in the living room. He looked comfortable, at home. He'd spread a sheet—*their sheet*—on the carpet, plumped a pillow, and he now stood to the side, waiting for her.

She experienced the sensation of air vanishing from the room.

Meghan turned off the flashlight, accidentally dropping the pillow. A part of her wished she'd kept the flashlight on. Only a single lantern burned, the weak flicker serving to make the surroundings more intimate.

While she sought to gather her scattered wits by finishing making up their makeshift bed, he stoked the fire, flashes of orange dancing across the ceiling and highlighting the subtle shadings of color in his dark hair.

Snowflake sauntered in and flopped down near the fire. Making a funny dog noise, he settled for the night.

After placing the metal guard across the fireplace, Kyle said, "That'll keep us warm."

Just being in his presence seemed to do that.

Meghan nervously folded her arms across her chest. Despite the fact she'd briefly been married, she had little experience with men. Kyle Murdock wasn't a thing like her ex-husband. In his presence, no element of fear had ever traced her spine.

Kyle's pervading presence was an entirely different story.

She watched, mesmerized by the ripple of corded muscle

as he lowered himself, drawing a blanket up to cover his lower body.

"I won't bite," Kyle said, a hint of laughter in his voice. He'd propped on his side, head supported by his upturned arm. "Unless you ask me to."

She froze on the spot.

"That was a joke, Meghan."

"I know," she fibbed, trying valiantly to vanquish the all-too-real image of him being that close, of being that intimate, of him feathering his lips across her skin.

What would his kiss feel like?

Warm? Moist?

Why did she care?

And worse, why did her insides cry out for it?

"Relax," he urged.

She wanted to leave on her robe for protection but didn't want him to see her cowardice. She told herself to act normally, then realized she didn't have a clue how to do that.

Fingers shaking, she fumbled with the knot cinching the material together.

Kyle watched. Instead of turning over and feigning sleep, giving her much-needed privacy, he watched.

The knot surrendered, the terry cloth gaped.

Her sleep shirt was conservative, with elbow-length sleeves and a hem that skirted her knees. And yet the recognition that skittered through her made her feel naked.

The air made her nipples tighten...at least she told herself it was the air, and not the scrutiny of the stranger camped several feet away.

Kyle pushed to a sitting position. He offered his hand. It was more than a physical crutch, she realized, it was an emotional one, too.

Aware of her state of nerves, Kyle, like the gentleman he'd promised to be, had obviously decided to help.

She accepted.

She was sinking, drowning in the multitudes of depths he possessed. Dangerous, yes, but wrapped in an appealing package that encouraged a woman to forget his lethal power.

Her hand slid inside his palm. He closed his fingers, and she noted his masculinity, his strength.

In pulse-pounding seconds, she was sitting next to him. After releasing her, he lay down, watched her with a miss-nothing gaze.

The fireplace cracked. She jumped.

Kyle lifted the blanket along with his brow.

Swallowing, she lowered herself, keeping a safe distance from him. Not that there was anything such as a safe distance from an imminent threat.

"Good night," she said, the words wavering as she turned on her side, presenting him with her backside.

She wasn't sure if she really heard his mocking laugh or if she only imagined it.

"Meghan?"

"Hmm?" she said around a pantomimed yawn.

"Come here."

Her blood thundered to a standstill.

"Sleeping five feet away from me defeats the purpose."

Her thoughts swam, and sensation after sensation skidded on top of one another.

She didn't move. But he did.

The firmness of his body snuggled hers. He nudged his knees behind hers, wrapped a hand around her middle and pulled her back a couple of inches. Meghan drank in a deep breath, reminding her heart to beat.

The back of her thighs rested against the hardness of muscle, the scrape of denim. His broad chest seemed to welcome the fit of her back. But it was his hand that bothered her most.

His palm rested on her middle, his fingers splayed on her ribs. He was so close to brushing her breast. So close...

A traitorous thought slipped past her defenses. She wanted...to touch, to damn the consequences, to embrace the danger. She stifled an instinctive moan, biting hard on the inside of her lip.

He would be gone soon, and she didn't need a second broken heart to nurse.

All his talk of Christmas had stirred up memories better left as bitter ashes. And they served as painful reminders. Trust only led to disillusionment.

So why did she want to accept his foolish promise to take away the hurt of Christmas past? Worse, why didn't she want to believe his promise to be a perfect gentleman?

"G'morning."

Kyle turned. The sight of his sleep-tousled bed partner made his insides tighten. She looked well rested. The brightness in her eyes served as a not-so-subtle reminder that while she'd enjoyed rest, he'd spent most of the night awake.

With her in his arms, and with his body's instinctive response and his damnable promises, sleep had been an elusive mistress.

"Is that breakfast?" she asked, the huskiness of sleep threading through her tone.

Absently he wondered if her voice contained the same sensual scratch during lovemaking. What would his name sound like, dragged around the breathy notes?

"Kyle?"

He forced his attention to what she'd said. "It's breakfast," he affirmed.

"Smells good." Meghan donned her robe and closed it at the waist, tugging the knot tight.

He wanted to untie it, let the lapels fall apart, then peel the thick terry cloth from her shoulders.

But he wouldn't.

He'd given his word.

Only God above knew how difficult it had been to keep *that* promise when her derriere had pressed, alluringly and temptingly, against his sex. Her hair had fanned across his chest while her cheek pressed against his bicep. As the night progressed and she absorbed some of his body heat, she shifted, the sleep shirt riding high on her thighs. He'd kept still, restrained his desire and focused on thoughts of teaching the lovely Meghan to believe in Christmas.

This morning, he was no closer to deciding how to accomplish that, either.

He turned back to the stove as she started to walk farther into the chilled kitchen. Her slippered feet made no sound on the ancient floor, but he was extremely aware of her presence, of the femininity that breezed into the room along with her.

When she joined him, Snowflake looked up, gave a soft whimper, then, anxious for more handouts, returned his attention to Kyle.

Meghan chuckled softly. "Snowflake has forgotten where his loyalties lie."

"No, he hasn't," Kyle countered. "Keeper of the kibbles is lord and master."

Meghan crouched to ruffle the dog's fur. Snowflake divided his attention between her and the stove.

Kyle glanced at her, noticing she looked up at him through those wide, trusting eyes. Her voice soft, she asked, "How did you sleep?"

"Like hell."

"Too cold?"

Too hot. He shook his head, returning his attention to

the stove. Picking up the pan, he shook the contents, then with a move of the wrist, flipped the omelette.

She pushed to a standing position, peeking in the pan. "I'm impressed."

"Don't be," he said. "Omelettes are the only thing I know how to make. Had to master something in college or starve."

She laughed, the sound hypnotizing his senses.

In fact, in barely twelve hours, the woman had pulverized his resistance and ignited feelings he didn't know existed. He'd never spent a night with an alluring woman without so much as a good-night kiss.

And damn it, he'd do it again, if it meant seeing a smile on her face.

He had to get the Harley started and hightail it back to Chicago. Fast.

Unfortunately the weather wasn't cooperating. Snow still tumbled from the heavens in ungodly amounts. Wind whipped the white stuff into a tornadolike frenzy, and the sun had yet to slash its way through the thick blanket of clouds.

"Did you make enough for two?" she asked, shattering the tension he felt and she probably hadn't even been aware of.

Kyle nodded. "Water's ready to boil, too. Thought you might want some tea. I made orange juice earlier, when I carried the stuff from the freezer and refrigerator to the barn. I figured it would stay colder out there since there's no electricity."

Hell, he'd had to do something physical to distract himself from the sight of her, the soft sounds of her sleeping. He'd dug out the Harley, moved it to the carport, brought in his saddlebag with fresh clothes and spent enough time under the water of a cool shower to dull his arousal.

Or so he'd thought.

She opened the refrigerator and the freezer doors simultaneously. After closing them, she asked, "You did all this?"

He shrugged. Addictive. Her approval was addictive. The more he got, the more he wanted. "Didn't think you wanted the perishables to thaw."

"You don't need to take care of me like this."

Meghan placed her hand on his arm. Oh, yeah. Addictive. "It needed to be done," he said.

"I think I'll keep you around."

He met her gaze. And for a second, just a crazy second, he wanted to stay.

Seeming to sense his intensity, and that perhaps she'd said more than she should, Meghan blinked and released her hold.

Probably better that she had; still, he wished she hadn't.

"I'll, er, set the table," Meghan stated, invading his body space again in order to access a cabinet. He moved to the side, not knowing how he'd react if she accidentally grazed him. The first touch had been difficult to let go of. The second might push his hard-won control over the edge.

Meghan looked out the back window as he'd done before any light had scattered across the frozen earth. "It looks worse this morning than it did last night," she said softly.

The kettle shrilled.

He turned off the flame, wishing his rampant feelings were as easy to extinguish. She deserved better. Deserved a houseguest who wasn't a liar. Deserved an honorable man whose every thought wasn't on touching her, holding her, kissing her.

"I guess this means you're still stranded," she said. He noticed her hand trembled as she pulled open a drawer and fished for silverware.

Was she as unnerved as he? "Unless you kick me out," he said, the words as much a statement as a question.

"No." She shook her head, her hair settling to frame her face as it might after his hands threaded through the strands. Concentrating on what she was doing, she quietly added, "You're welcome to stay until the roads are passable."

He wondered if he would survive it.

Within several seconds, he'd halved the omelette and slid a portion onto her plate. Kyle poured hot water on top of her tea bag, then joined her at the table.

She kept conversation general; he followed her lead.

Then all of a sudden, she leveled her gaze at him. He felt as if he'd been nailed between the eyes with a two-by-four.

"Where were you heading?"

"Chicago," he answered. He didn't add the second part, the word that had always followed Chicago. *Home.* Chicago didn't seem like home anymore.

"And where are you coming from?"

He shrugged, then decided he had nothing to gain by not answering. "California."

She moved aside her plate, leaving a large part of her food untouched. No wonder she was so thin. It occurred to him again that she needed a keeper. He reminded himself it would have to be someone else.

His future was carefully mapped out.

She studied him intently, as if trying to decide how much to ask, how much was her business.

"You took a motorcycle trip in December?"

He nodded.

She licked her lower lip as she toyed with her spoon. Then she drew a shallow breath. "Were you running or were you hiding?"

He flinched.

She put down her spoon and continued to regard him.

No coward there, he marveled. He admired her guts. "No one else has asked me that."

In fact, when he'd stated his intention of hitting the road for a month, his father had frowned, adding a couple of comments regarding Kyle's mental state. He'd even hinted that maybe Kyle wasn't equal to the honor his father wanted to bestow.

The only other person who cared was Pamela. She'd made him promise to be there when Raymond and Whitney woke on Christmas morning.

Meghan patiently waited.

He stalled.

Then he reminded himself of her hospitality, of the fact she knew next to nothing about him. And he recalled the pain in her voice when she'd told him of her past.

"Running." His voice was rough, dragged from someplace he didn't have the guts to face.

Wrapping her hands around her cup, she asked, "Am I harboring a criminal?"

"A criminal?" he echoed. Seeing her seriousness, he added, "No."

"I didn't think so."

Another few seconds of silence followed before she spoke again. "Then, who or what are you running from?"

Kyle swallowed.

"Kyle?"

"My life," he admitted rawly.

With that painful realization, he stood, not caring that his chair crashed to the floor behind him.

Five

Meghan watched as he shrugged into his jacket and turned up the collar with clipped, controlled motions. He shoved his feet into stiff, wet leather boots, all without saying a word.

"I didn't mean to pry," she said, wondering how to best make amends but suspecting he wouldn't even appreciate it.

The man was obviously a loner.

He'd said he was running from his life. She didn't have much knowledge of men on the run, but it was a good bet he had something to hide or hide from.

It shouldn't matter to her. Yet it did. She should act like a polite stranger until the roads were cleared. But she couldn't.

"Kyle?"

Not looking at her, he turned the doorknob, a flurry blasting through the opening. Within seconds, he sealed the door behind him, closing out the cold, separating them.

Goose bumps traveling the length of her arms, she hugged her chest and crossed to the window. He fought the elements, grabbing a shovel and reclearing the path he'd obviously worked through earlier. His movements were powerful but abrupt as he threw snow on top of already-drifted piles.

Even from a distance, and beneath leather, she noted his strength, the same strength that had originally frightened her, but the same strength that was capable of great tenderness, as she had experienced last night. He'd encouraged her to relax and slowly she had. As apprehension faded, he'd used that strength to protect her, cradling her and offering his body as a shield against the chill.

Meghan absently reached for her clay angel and traced the halo. "Well, Lexie, looks like I blew it. Mr. Murdock doesn't want to talk about himself."

Lexie's serene smile didn't waver.

With a sigh, Meghan returned the angel to the counter and opened the faucet, glad the water heater wasn't electric. Even though she tried not to, she glanced back out the window.

Several events slipped by, seemingly in slow motion, each frame frozen in time. Horrified, she watched, unable to force her stunned body into action.

Obviously frightened by Kyle's sudden appearance, Aspen, Meghan's old, normally docile horse, crashed through the barn door. With a whinny, Aspen reared.

Kyle raised his hands to protect his head from thrashing hooves.

He slipped on a sheet of ice, hitting the ground hard. His curse ricocheted across the frosty air.

Meghan headed for the back door, barely remembering to turn off the rushing water.

She stuffed her bare feet into boots and belted her robe

more tightly. Rushing, Meghan battled the wind to force open the door. "Kyle!"

Thankfully Aspen moved away from him and tentatively backed into the wide-open barn, but Kyle didn't answer. Worse, he didn't move.

Fear pounded through her. Blizzard-force snow stung her face, cold bit at her ears, in seconds her fingers felt numb. "Kyle!" she called again. There was no response except for the eerie howl of wind and the sound of the barn door slapping against the weathered exterior wall.

Damn it. She'd known the barn door was unstable, and Aspen's stall hadn't latched tightly for nearly a year. If anything serious happened to Kyle because of her negligence, Meghan would never forgive herself.

Slipping and sliding, she hurried to his side. Guilt waged war with fear as she dropped to her knees. "Don't move," she said quietly when Kyle dug his elbows into the snow and tried to push to a sitting position.

"Get back..." He coughed. "Inside."

Ignoring his command, she brushed back hair from his forehead. "Where are you hurt?"

"Meghan, you're hardly dressed. You're going to catch a cold if you don't do what I—"

"I'm not leaving you here, Kyle. You're stuck with me."

They glared at each other for frigid moments. She wasn't backing down, and the sooner he realized it, the better.

"Stubborn woman."

"Where are you hurt?" she repeated, looking anxiously to assure herself it wasn't serious.

"I'm fine, just winded."

"Kyle," she warned.

"My head."

Gently she probed with her fingertips, stopping when she found a knot and he winced. Fortunately there didn't seem to be any cuts.

"Help me...sit up."

She debated her options. She wasn't sure he should move, but he definitely couldn't be left on the freezing ground. After standing, she bent to offer her hand.

He accepted.

She drew her lower lip between her teeth, biting hard so as not to say anything about the sight of his split knuckles. Cold crept up her clothing, shooting shivers through her.

"Didn't tell me the horse was a maniac," he said.

"Aspen?" she asked, exerting a small amount of pressure to slowly help him. "She's usually as mild-mannered—"

"As professional athletes in the playoffs."

She couldn't manage a smile for his benefit. "I'm sorry, I should have warned you about the door."

"My fault. I'd noticed earlier." He inhaled sharply. "I was going to fix it."

His pale features concerned her. She had to get him inside. Fast. "Here, put your arm around my shoulder."

He did as she instructed, then groaned as she took the first, gingerly placed step toward the house. She shortened the next step, encouraging him to lean more heavily on her.

"My angel."

His comment gave her momentary pause. Angel. She liked the sound of it. Instead of letting her mind play with the thought, she said, "We'll both be heavenly inhabitants if we don't get out of the elements."

Once the door was slammed behind them, she helped Kyle into a kitchen chair. Gnawing her lower lip, she filled a glass bowl with water, then took a towel from the bottom drawer.

Her heart thundered as she shivered, as much from fear as the cold. Returning to him, she offered silent hopes that he didn't need more medical assistance than she could provide.

He unfastened his jacket, the surrendering zipper shredding the quiet. Meghan knelt to help him remove sodden boots, wishing she wasn't so very aware of him. This close, sensations she didn't dare name zinged through her.

"Better," he said when his second boot joined the first on the floor.

"Let me take a look at your hand."

"It's nothing," he protested.

"So humor me."

"Lady, there's nothing I'd like more."

Their gazes collided. And held. With a deep swallow, she looked away and busied herself dipping the cloth into the bowl. After wringing it out, she reached for his hand, resting his fingers in the palm of hers.

Cold against cold.

Then a gradual warming.

The act wasn't medical, she realized. Nurses didn't, or shouldn't, have such a physical response to a patient. But her response was definitely physical, and even more frightening, emotional.

She'd confided in him last night, baring a part of her soul she'd never before revealed...to anyone. With him, the sharing seemed natural. Maybe it was because she knew she'd never see him again.

Maybe it was something more.

And he'd revealed, albeit reluctantly, a part of himself—raising the emotional risks for both of them.

Refusing to follow that thought further, she dabbed his knuckles with the warm water. He flinched. Instantly she eased the pressure. "How's that?"

He nodded. "Good."

"Anywhere else hurt?"

"My pride."

She smiled slightly and glanced heavenward, offering her silent thanks.

Meghan stood, went to the cabinet and took down some antibacterial ointment. She slowly crossed back to him, cognizant of how devastatingly handsome he was. Color had returned to his face and broad shoulders filled out the cotton material.

From a single glance, she recalled, in astounding detail from the night before, the nuances that lay beneath five small buttons.

She knelt in front of him, ignoring the scent of untamed male that he seemed to own. Struggling for concentration, Meghan uncapped the tube and once again took his injured hand in hers.

Easing the slick ointment across his skin was an intimacy that shouldn't have disturbed her as much as it did.

"Thank you," he said.

Meghan slowly looked up.

Their gazes locked.

She swallowed.

His eyes had narrowed, the deep blue color darkening with an intensity her feminine intuition instantly comprehended.

Beware.

He was no longer the patient. Instead, he was a man who didn't need her help. He was once again a take-charge male, the kind that made her infinitely aware of being his opposite—as nature intended.

"Meghan?"

"How's your head?" she asked inanely, hoping to shatter the growing bond that had every intuitive sense on heightened awareness.

"It's been bumped before."

Before she had a chance to respond, he turned the tables. He captured both her hands in his, then pulled her gently toward him, bringing her into the cradle of his thighs.

He didn't blink, keeping the tension taut.

She wanted...

Wanted not to want.

His hand holding her chin prisoner, he leaned forward, his face only a few hesitant inches from her own.

Years of deprivation, hunger for human touch—if only fleeting—surged in her.

"You're freezing," he said.

"Aftermath of adrenaline."

"You're freezing," he said again, "because you rescued me."

She no longer felt cold; in fact, heat seeped through all of her, leaving awakening in its trail. Danger consumed her.

"I appreciate it, Meghan, appreciate you." His lips brushed hers.

She sucked in a breath, meeting his touch and silently, with her body if not words, asking for more. So much more.

His lips skimmed across hers a second time.

It wasn't enough. Oh, Lord help her, it wasn't nearly enough.

He pulled back slightly. Instinctively, she swayed toward him.

Kyle's smile was enigmatic, and her resistance did a corresponding slow melt.

He stood, drawing her along with him. Her nipples tightened, hardened. In all her years, she'd never felt this...womanly before. When he released her hands, she rested a palm against his chest, feeling the rapid pulsation of his heart.

Kyle's body showed he was as affected as she.

She liked that.

"Meghan." Her name floated on a breath of air, sounding silky, sweet. Then he said it again, and a shudder of surprise traced her spine.

This time her name sounded rough, broken into two syllables that held a distinctively desperate edge.

He wanted, too.

She rose on her tiptoes, allowed her hands to ease across the cotton of his deep blue flannel shirt. The material was soft, but underneath, his muscles lay powerful and strong. She imagined the mat of hair covering his chest, then allowed her hands to wander, wrapping around him. She touched the hair at his nape, savoring the texture, rich, thick and tantalizing.

Kyle's hand splayed across her back, covering her from shoulder blade to shoulder blade. She felt safe in his arms, just like she had last night…shielded and cherished.

Her eyelids drifted closed as he took her lips.

A tease.

A sigh.

A tempting nip.

A groan.

His tongue sought entrance. She surrendered, opening her mouth, meeting his taste.

Her emotions quivered along with her insides. She shouldn't trust, shouldn't be doing this, shouldn't think of anything but the repercussions.

She shoved away the intrusive thoughts. His hand stroked her, settling on her tailbone. She didn't pull away; instead, she responded, reaching out with her tongue, seeking his. Kyle exerted subtle pressure, bringing them even closer.

Hard.

He was hard. So very hard.

And with that realization, reality intruded.

She ended the kiss, then swallowed. He held her for a few more seconds while she sought to piece together her shattered equilibrium.

She never behaved this way.

Loneliness shouldn't matter. She'd been lonely for years. That didn't mean she should surrender to the first man who happened along, particularly if that man was a loner, running from his life.

He wasn't the type of man she should find attractive.

The fact she did frightened her more than the aura of mystery that surrounded him.

Afraid of what he might think of her, Meghan pressed her fingers across her kiss-swollen lips, took a step backward, then rushed from the room.

"Oh. Oh, my."

Lexie cracked her bubblegum. "Well," she said to Grandma Aggie, "the first part of our mission is accomplished." Lexie gave a satisfied smile. Her charge was...how did she use to say it...twitterpated, and things appeared to be progressing as well as she'd hoped.

Lexie checked the watch that hung from a golden chain. "Right on schedule."

"But the snow..."

"We'll give the clouds one last squeeze."

"But was it really necessary for my Kyle to get hurt?" Grandma Aggie protested, just as she had repeatedly during the past twelve Earth hours. "That was an awful hard fall he took."

Lexie blew a bubble, then let it pop. "It wasn't as hard as it was supposed to be."

"Well I couldn't stand here and do nothing," Aggie protested.

"Lexie!"

The voice boomed from within and without. Trouble. In capital letters and punctuated by an exclamation point. Lexie swallowed her gum. Fluttering her wings, she leaned closer to Aggie and conspiratorially whispered, "Squeeze the clouds."

"But Lexie—"

"I'm in trouble, and you're not being watched." She

winked, acting braver than she actually felt. In truth, the silver dusting on her wings shivered. "And remind that grandson of yours that it's Christmas."

Kyle dug his fingers into his hair, wincing when he irritated the bump on his scalp.

Damn.

He was a fool. A thousand times.

Why the hell had he kissed her? He should have kept his hands to himself. Yet rational thought was all but impossible when she was near.

Still, nothing made up for the fact he'd abused her generosity.

Or that he'd do it again in less time than it took to draw a breath.

Meghan Carroll was a desirable woman. But he'd been around a dozen desirable women at a party a little more than a month ago. He hadn't kissed a single one of them.

So what was it about her?

Logic told him to get away. Hike through the snow. Try the reluctant Harley a second time.

Yet a glance outside spoke of futility.

He was stranded. And he found the courage to face a painful realization. He owed Meghan an explanation—he who never explained a damn thing to anyone. He'd been rude before he went outside, repaying her hospitality with hostility.

She deserved better.

Deserved honesty.

Automatically he cleaned up the mess she'd made while caring for him.

Caring.

Yeah, that word described her.

Caring. She cared about an old mutt, a horse that should have been sold for glue, and even worse, a stranded man.

And she cared about her house, along with the carefully carved angel....

Kyle reached for the winged cherub. Lexie. That's what Meghan had called the guardian. He traced his thumbnail across the halo, remembering again the grandmother who'd meant so much to him and the uncanny resemblance the sculpture had to Grandma Aggie.

She'd been a caring individual also; he'd been lucky to have her in his life.

And Meghan...he'd been lucky to have her in his life, also.

He heard her footsteps upstairs. Pacing. In her bedroom? Her studio?

Kyle wanted to talk, but, judging by the expression on her face when she'd left the kitchen—tightly compressed lips, wide hazel eyes shaded by a hint of disbelief and shock—she wouldn't appreciate the intrusion.

The kiss had shaken him. And from the speed with which she'd pivoted and run, it had had an equal effect on her.

He recalled the feel of her, her nipples against his chest, her back beneath his palm.

They would fit together.

Oh, yeah.

Like Christmas and mistletoe.

Their kiss had been as natural as it was inevitable.

And even though he probably should, he wouldn't apologize.

He wanted her. Holding her in his arms all night, her alluring behind wiggled against his pelvis, had been barely this side of torture.

It'd been agony; it'd been pleasure.

He expelled a breath of air.

Deciding to give her some time alone while he figured out his next step and tried to undo some of the damage he'd wreaked, Kyle went into the living room.

Crouching, he rubbed his hands together and stared into the dwindling fire, lost in images of her. Smiling. Frowning. Teasing. Nibbling her lip.

Excited.

She'd responded to him, woman to man.

She fired feelings of possessiveness and protectiveness, feelings no other female, anywhere, anytime, had inspired.

He wanted to take care of her, and not just to repay the favors she'd granted him. In fact, he'd spent a good portion of the early morning hours fulfilling that desire.

Trying to keep up with the snow, he'd shoveled the walks and driveway. Then he managed to push the stubborn Beast into the carport, and moved the refrigerator and freezer items to the barn. He'd checked the faucets, opening an outside one a fraction of a turn, allowing water to trickle so the pipes wouldn't burst. Inside, he'd prepared breakfast and couldn't remember ever feeling so...domestic.

The experience should have been alien. Instead, it felt natural. Seductive. Impossible.

He picked up the poker and stabbed at the embers smoldering in the fireplace. After rearranging them, he tossed another log on top.

Having no idea how long it might take her to come back downstairs, and unaccustomed to inaction of any kind, Kyle tugged on his boots, pulled on his coat and headed along the slick walk to the barn.

The snow was slowly diminishing, and the clouds seemed to be parting. Maybe within a few hours, the sun would triumph over the not-predicted storm, relegating it to the annals of history.

Kyle looked back at the house, seeing the shadow of her silhouette in the window. She raised her hand in a half greeting; he saluted. When he glanced back again, she was gone. The barn door hung jaggedly from disjointed hinges.

First things first. He would repair the door, then worry about the crazy horse, who was now standing by the corral.

Kyle strode to a shelf, finding the tools he needed to repair the door—screws, screwdriver, new hinges.

Nearly an hour later, the wind abruptly died, as if it had blown itself out. Quiet serenity cloaked the landscape, snow stopped drifting, and a watery ray of sunshine poked through a small slit in a gray cloud.

Kyle's mood didn't lift along with the weather. After putting Aspen back in her stall, he hunted for a saw, a chisel, then scrounged a couple dozen nails and found a hammer.

He closed his fist around the wooden handle, testing the weight of the metal head. This felt right. And now, with the path his future was mapped on, the yearning to build and create would become nothing more than a hobby.

He softly swore. Then, reminding himself the trip had been planned to get the demons out of his system, that he'd be fine once he reached Chicago, he studied the piece of wood in front of him.

Placing the chisel, he tapped the end with the hammer.

Exorcise the demons? Right.

Still, the gift he intended to create might not be much, but it would serve as a Christmas present for the angel who'd rescued him from the cold—Lord knew, she'd apparently received too few gifts in her life.

And he knew she would accept this...even if she didn't want his kiss.

Six

Darn it to pieces.

She couldn't concentrate. Couldn't think. Kyle Murdock had charged into her life and turned every part upside down.

Meghan paced, stopping in front of the window. Again. She'd done that repeatedly over the last few hours, even though she ordered herself not to.

She glanced toward the barn for the hundredth time that morning. The huge set of double doors stood closed, leaving her unable to see anything, or anyone.

A specific anyone.

Kyle.

Like a woman sensually starved, she'd watched his every move as he'd repaired the door. After the first few minutes, he'd removed his jacket. A little later, he'd paused, tipped back his head and wiped a forearm across his brow, despite the absence of sun or warmth.

Afterward, he had emerged from the barn, carrying a hammer, and headed toward a downed rail on the corral.

Aspen had ventured toward Kyle, which made Meghan's heart flip over. She'd twisted her hands together, wondering if she should go outside, but Kyle had looked up from what he was doing, frozen on the spot, and stood with his legs braced apart.

Hesitantly, Aspen had moved forward. Kyle had remained rooted as Aspen stretched out and nudged his pocket, in search of a treat. Kyle had caved in, stroking his fingers down the animal's nose.

Meghan had imagined, rather than heard, Aspen's whinny of approval.

And in that instant, Meghan had realized she was in a tremendous amount of trouble.

Any man who treated her animals like that, especially after nearly being crushed...

With his nose, Snowflake pushed open the door and strolled in. He waited for Meghan to pet him, then curled up in front of the hearth. Resolutely, Meghan tamped down her feelings for Kyle and turned her back on the window. Lost in thought, she added another piece of pine to the fire.

The heat from burning logs was usually adequate to keep the chill away while she worked, but not today. The heavy sweater and winter-weight leggings didn't help, either. In all honesty, Meghan knew she hadn't felt warm since she ran up the stairs...away from Kyle and the multitude of emotions cascading through her since he kissed her.

It bothered her that she'd responded so freely. It bothered her even more that she'd follow him again, even if the only place he was leading was straight into temptation.

Frustration growing, she returned to her table and tried to work.

The pink on the angel's cheeks didn't look believable—too dark. And the eyebrows she'd placed were too thick, too close together. As if the angel were frowning.

Frowning?

Her angels never, ever expressed Meghan's personal emotions. At least they hadn't until now. Kyle hadn't been under her roof for twenty-four hours and already he'd shaken her, tantalized her, compelled her to experience emotions she'd thought long gone and buried.

She had to stay busy.

Mindlessly, she pulled on the headphones of her stereo cassette player and began tying tiny bows out of satin ribbons. She would need bows, whenever she managed to complete another angel, even though that didn't seem likely to happen today.

A knock on the door made her jump. Snowflake raised his head, cocking it to one side.

She turned down the volume and heard another knock.

"Meghan?"

Her heart thundered a few extra beats into its normal rhythm. No one had ever trespassed the sanctuary of her studio. She shouldn't let Kyle in. Wouldn't. "Just a minute!"

The knob turned and six-foot-plus of power and potency dominated her private domain.

Fingers nerveless, she slowly removed the headset.

"We need to talk."

She struggled to find a light, airy attitude. But being superficial didn't suit her. Instead, she pulled up her legs onto the chair and wrapped her arms around them.

He radiated tension and passion. Her insides became a molten river of need. Instinctively, her body craved what her mind refused to acknowledge.

"I won't apologize for kissing you."

Oxygen escaped her lungs.

"Because I'm not a hypocrite. I'd kiss you again. And again."

Meghan met his eyes, eyes whose blue color had darkened to that of a Colorado alpine lake as the sun was setting. "Kyle, please."

He dragged his fingers into his hair. "But I do owe you an explanation for my behavior this morning."

"You don't owe me anything," she softly said, suddenly aware of the dwarfed proportions of the room. "You're a houseguest until the roads clear, I don't have a right to intrude on—"

"Damn it, Meghan, you do have a right." He strode to the window and tapped his fingers against the casing. "And at this point, I'm more than a houseguest."

"No," she said to his back. "You're not." She wondered if she was trying to convince him, or herself. Forcing a lie and hoping she didn't choke on the words, Meghan continued, "A kiss doesn't mean anything."

He swung around in a lethally swift motion. "No?" he demanded, throwing her words back in her face.

She gulped.

"You kiss every man who happens along?"

Wondering how this conversation had gotten so out of hand so quickly, she shook her head.

"And those you do kiss, do you respond to them so thoroughly?" His words were soft and simultaneously saber sharp.

Cutting.

She ran her tongue across her teeth.

"I didn't think so."

He hadn't taken a single step toward her, for which she was eternally grateful. Thinking straight when he stood across the room proved difficult. And if he'd pulled her into his arms like he had earlier, Meghan knew she would come undone. As much as she wanted to deny her response, she couldn't. It shook her, forced her to question everything she'd always taken for granted.

"No lies, Meghan. Not between us."

Us.

Had he placed a subtle emphasis on the word or had she merely imagined it? She wanted to say there was no "us," but that would add another check mark in the "lies" column.

No matter what, she would never forget him. And for this brief flash of time, where the world was winter-wonderland white and the future blocked by a blizzard of snow, they were together.

While a casual affair wasn't in her nature, loneliness was a companion she would willingly take a break from.

"I was rude earlier," Kyle continued.

"Forget it," she said quietly. "I have. I don't usually pry."

"You weren't prying. You asked a fair question." Kyle paused, digging his fingers shallowly into his hair. He winced, obviously scraping across his injury.

She wrapped her arms more firmly around her legs.

"I said no lies, and walking away without a reason is tantamount to a lie."

His tone had dropped to an intimate whisper on crackling air. She read openness and undisguised candor in his eyes and realized with a start that Kyle was entrusting her with a part of himself.

"You were right, I was running. I've been on the road about a month."

She remained silent while he pivoted and stared out the window again.

"My father is Miles Murdock."

"Of Murdock Enterprises?" She arched a surprised eyebrow.

"One and the same." He faced her again. "You've heard of us?"

"My parents own stock."

"Miles intends to retire at the end of the year."

Miles, not Dad or Father. Miles.

"I'm his heir apparent," he said with as much enthusiasm as if he were scheduled to face a firing squad at dawn.

"And you don't want the position." Recognition dawned on her. "You said you were on your way to Chicago. Home."

"Home?" His full lips, so sensual earlier, formed a sneer. "Hardly."

"You'll do it even though you don't want to."

Kyle folded his arms across his chest, stretching the soft cotton of his shirt tight. "It's my responsibility."

"You won't turn your back?"

"No." His word was as frigid as the ice hanging from the porch roof.

She rested her chin on top of her knees, admiring his sense of obligation, knowing it was what made him the man he was—the man she'd trusted without logical reason. Still, living a shattered dream couldn't be easy. "I'm sorry."

"It's my duty." He shrugged, but she read his control, noted the absence of passion he usually exuded.

With a flash of chilling insight, Meghan realized that the Kyle who so thoroughly commanded her space wouldn't be the same man in Chicago.

The thought bothered her, even though realistically it wasn't her concern.

Somehow, somewhere along the line, Kyle had become her concern.

He pushed away from the window, his footsteps drowned by the thundering of her pulse.

"Apology accepted?" he asked.

She tipped back her head, meeting his gaze. "None needed."

Having seen it once before and surrendering to its magic, Meghan recognized the glint of purposefulness in his eye.

She pulled her legs more tightly to her chest.

He offered his hand. She considered, discarding her brain's logical suggestion to ignore it. Instead, as if latching on to something very special, she accepted his hand, unfolding her legs and standing, allowing him to tug her closer. And closer. Near him she felt unbelievably small, but not threatened.

The few hours apart had been nearly as awful as the night before, lying in his arms, so close, yet so far away. She'd been emotionally starved for so long that, until Kyle's arrival, she hadn't realized how empty her life was.

Sleep had been elusive the first few hours. His body had warmed hers, but her imagination kept her awake, taunting her with thoughts of what it might be like to have a man desire her again, truly want her.

His earlier kiss had given her a glimpse of that possibility. She'd liked it. Oh, how she'd liked it.

And Meghan realized she wanted more.

"You're a special woman, Meghan."

Color, hot, fast and furious, rushed to her face. She wasn't special, she was wanton.

"I said I wanted to kiss you again, Meghan. But I changed my mind," he said, releasing her hand to cradle her face between his palms.

She knit her eyebrows.

"I want *you* to kiss me."

Molten need flared into fire.

He wanted her to kiss him. Embarrassment swirled into the tumultuous blend of feelings. She'd never taken the initiative before, wasn't quite sure how to act, how to react. She blinked, not knowing how to admit the truth. "I…"

"You lead," he said quietly into the silence she'd left, his gaze holding her captive.

She couldn't look away if she wanted, and she realized she didn't want to.

"I frightened you earlier."

Meghan shook her head, but couldn't reveal the truth. Her own reaction scared her, not Kyle—never Kyle. Stalling, she licked her lower lip and noted the way his eyes banked with an emotion she dared not name.

Seeming to sense what she couldn't fathom, he leaned toward her a fraction of an inch. Within seconds, he could have claimed her mouth. Yet he didn't. He'd given her control.

As if drawn by an inexorable spell, she eased toward him. Tension zinged. She was so aware of the feel of his hands on her skin, against her cheek, and of his strength that protected.

He stroked his right thumb down her jaw, feathered the fingers of his left hand into the layers of her hair.

This felt so…right.

Nerves frazzled and excited, she accepted his offer and took control.

She allowed her lips to light across his. The touch was glancing, nothing more than a tease. And still, it possessed the power to curl her bare toes into the carpeting.

She did it a second time, feeding her internal need.

His breath mingled with hers…warmth and promise wrapped as a gift she wanted desperately to unwrap.

Kyle's hands dropped onto her shoulders, and she seized the opportunity to reach up and place her palms on his face. She felt chiseled, blunt features. The shading on his unshaven chin scratched her hands, adding a second tactile assault.

She rocked forward onto her tiptoes, slanting her lips across his, seeking entry as he had earlier, before she'd fled.

This time, Meghan knew she wouldn't be running anywhere.

His hands tightened on her shoulders in timed harmony with the meeting of their tongues.

She probed his mouth, moist heat mating with moist heat. How had she thought, for even one irrational moment, that she could control the kiss?

Resolve splintered.

She started to unravel, a shudder sliding the length of her spine. Tingling demand flowed through her as she deepened the kiss.

His ragged breathing seemed to come from a great distance, and she was no longer capable of logical thought. She arched forward, her breasts pressing against his chest. Her nipples had become hardened knots of need, and between her thighs, she throbbed.

Kyle groaned.

Her fingers tangled in his hair, and their dance, so imitative of lovemaking, continued, driving her to the brink. Physical and emotional reaction became a roller coaster, crashing her through dizzying highs and sharp twists and turns.

His grip on her had tightened, and his upper body effortlessly supported her weight.

The kiss they'd shared earlier didn't compared to this.

Kyle pulled back slightly and she became aware of his rigid stance and of the definitive bulge against her abdomen.

"Meghan," he said, breath hissing between his clenched teeth.

Heeding his unspoken warning—they were trespassing in the area of no return—she sought to school her sensual response, finding control difficult. It had flashed and flared, leaving her as adrift as a snowflake on the wind.

Releasing her hold on him, she stepped away and nervously dragged her fingers through her hair, realizing the strands had tangled beneath his touch.

Kyle moved away, resuming his spot near the window.

"I'm sorry," she whispered, trailing her fingers down her cheek, her skin sensitized from his shadow. "I didn't mean for it to go—" she drew a breath and finished "—so far."

"Don't apologize, damn it." His words were diamond-edge rough.

They'd gone further than she intended, past the point she'd ever felt comfortable with before. She'd flirted with the danger, and unbelievably, and just as undeniably, wanted to embrace it full on.

This wasn't like her. Jack had never elicited this type of yearning from her, and she'd married him.

Meghan struggled for solid footing, yet didn't quite know how to act. Her heart hammered and her nerve endings still tingled. And still she had to find something to say to divert herself so she didn't beg Kyle to take her in his arms again.

She sat in her chair, tucking her legs under her. The distance didn't help, though, not when he still seemed to suck the oxygen from the air and replace it with simmering sexual energy.

Near them, the fireplace cracked and hissed. Snowflake shifted his big body, yawned, stretched, then padded to Kyle's side. Traitorous mutt.

"Thanks for all your help around here," she said, thinking the words sounded rushed and, worse, inane, a tangible extension of her internal turmoil.

Absently, Kyle scratched Snowflake behind the ears, then he looked at her. His eyes were still darkened from desire; she wildly wondered if hers were, too.

"It was nothing."

"Nothing?" she asked. "Just a lot of chores I've been meaning to get done since last spring."

"Consider it repayment."

"I don't need or want repaying," she asserted.

He shrugged, effectively ending the topic, as if he'd sensed her attempt to make idle conversation. "I assume this is your studio?"

"And you're my first guest."

"Off limits?"

Quietly, she said, "It used to be."

"I feel privileged."

"Don't." In the same tone she added, "You weren't invited."

He nodded.

"No offense meant," she said.

"None taken." He moved toward the shelving unit covering a wall.

She swallowed. Her heart continued its frantic beat, this time from a feeling of exposure and vulnerability.

Not only was her studio private, so was her work. Only the best angels were taken into the neighboring towns and offered for sale. But here, all her efforts adorned the shelves, the ones she was most proud of sitting alongside the ones on whose faces she hadn't been able to capture true emotion.

"You did all of these?" Kyle looked at her and, with his thumb, indicated the dozens of angels.

Meghan nodded, twisting her hands together in her lap.

"You've gotten better and better."

Her insides warmed. To her, work was intensely personal, a reflection of her inner self. Approval for her clay angels was approval for her as a person—something she'd had little of through the years. She couldn't express how deeply his opinion mattered.

He'd turned away, hopefully hadn't noticed the way color spilled across her cheeks.

"No two are alike."

"That's my favorite part." She stood. Fighting against the inner voice that warned her to stay away, she went to him. He'd chosen her favorite topic. Enthusiasm bubbled over, extinguishing the threat of danger. She pulled two from the shelf, set them side by side on her palm. Even though they were the same design, named Winter Magic, there were subtle differences. "They each have an individual personality."

He took them from her, held them up and compared them. "One's a boy and one's a girl."

She arched a brow even as a smile sneaked past her defenses. "Kyle!"

"One's got a pink bow, and the other has a blue bow." This time he arched a brow. "How else would you tell them apart?"

Meghan plucked the angels from his hand and slid them back into place, noting she needed to dust.

"You said you're overstocked because of the storm?"

Last year, she'd had a banner time, right before Christmas. "I usually sell a lot as last-minute stocking stuffers. This year..." Her enthusiasm waned, and she trailed off.

"I'll buy fifty."

Her jaw dropped. "Fifty?"

"I have a lot of stockings to stuff."

"They're not cheap," she warned, trying to recover from shock.

"I didn't expect they were."

Her eyes narrowed. "Kyle, you're not...I mean, just because we—"

"No," he said in response to her unasked question. He swung toward her, capturing her shoulders in his hands. "I'm buying them because I want them. Because I think they'll be a welcome gift."

She looked up into his eyes, read the earnest expression,

and more…barely concealed passion. Her breaths became irregular.

"And because they'll be a reminder of a very special woman. And a special time."

"Still, you don't need fifty."

"Yes," he said. "I do."

His warmth seeped through her sweater, bringing a sweeping remembrance of their passion only a few moments ago. Unbelievably she wanted more, felt a desperate yearning to fall into his embrace, feel him, hard against soft, touch him, inhale his scent of honesty and belief.

"And I'll have you ship several dozen more to me. My sister runs a small gift shop in Chicago. She's always looking for new products. They'll be a hit. Before you know it, you'll have hundreds of orders to fill."

"I—" she drew a deep breath "—don't know how to thank you."

His eyes darkened. His breathing pattern altered.

She shuddered with recognition, suddenly knowing he'd thought of a way.

Seven

"**I**'d forgotten I still had a bottle of wine in the fridge," Meghan said.

"I found it when I took your stuff out to the barn this morning."

She set the table while he rooted in her junk drawer. He didn't have a junk drawer at home. Another one of those touches that made a house a home. And a second reminder of the lack in his own life.

Finally finding the corkscrew, he turned it into the neck of the bottle.

"We need more candles, otherwise we won't be able to see what I cooked." She wrinkled her nose. "Not that that would be all bad."

"Over there," he said, pointing to a drawer.

"In that drawer? Really?"

She needed a keeper.

For the dozenth time that day, he took the nagging

thought and tried to hide it from his conscience. Yeah, she needed a keeper, but he didn't intend to fill out any applications.

It wouldn't be long until he coaxed the Beast back to life. As soon as the storm blew itself out, crews would make the roads passable. He'd be home for Christmas. And this brief interlude with Meghan would become nothing more than a distant memory.

Sure. And his Harley would sprout wings and wear a pink garter.

With a vicious yank, he forced the bottle to release the cork.

Meghan Carroll had gotten to him. Hard and fast. She'd penetrated his ice-encased defenses, her soft, surrendering lips causing havoc he'd yet to sort through.

She opened a cabinet and reached toward the top shelf, dragging her sweater high on her hips, showing the length of her legs.

"Here," he said, coming up behind her. His thighs pushed against her, and Meghan's enticing derriere pressed into him. His body's instinctive response was as undeniably real as it was unwelcome.

Being near her was becoming more and more difficult with each hour. Keeping his hands to himself wasn't something he wanted to do. Instead, he longed to take her in his arms, kiss her the way God intended a woman to be kissed. But Kyle didn't have the right.

He'd be gone soon.

And he'd leave her behind. The idea of Meghan alone and lonely made his gut constrict. She was made for a partner. Made for a man. Made for—

Ruthlessly he cut off the thought and took down two glasses, desperate to get the hell away.

She swallowed deeply. Even in the dim light he saw the soft color that painted her cheeks. She drew breaths in short, uneven bursts, and beneath her sweater, he noticed her just-as-real reaction to him.

Kyle turned, then, beneath warm water, rinsed a layer of dust from the wineglasses. He poured for both of them, splashing more than was prudent into his own goblet.

Didn't alcohol dull the senses?

He cupped his hand around one of the glasses, offering her the base. Her fingertips brushed his, lightly, femininely, without wiles.

He recalled the feel of her skin as she'd trailed down his unshaven cheek, and the sound of the slight rasp.

What was it about this woman, he wondered, that was so special? He'd known plenty of women in his life, had been involved in long-term relationships. One, with Susan, had been serious and painful. But even Susan, whom he'd thought of marrying, hadn't affected him in such a profoundly powerful way.

He hadn't lain awake at night, holding Susan and worrying how she would manage without him. Last night, with Meghan, he'd had the experience.

And that disturbed him.

"Wine's good," she said, her oddly haunting voice slipping past his defenses.

He took a drink of his, the flavor of the white grapes a bit sweet, but it was better than nothing. Any blunting effect would be welcome.

Their kisses hadn't sated his appetite, rather they whetted his need for more. Even though logic coldly informed him to run like hell while an escape still existed, another, more primitive emotion urged him closer and closer. The thrill of being with Meghan compared to that of being on the Beast and taking a mountain curve too fast, too low, and too close to the edge.

The thrill of danger was worth the risk.

As long as he didn't hurt her.

Meghan carried the tapered candles to the table. He heard the snap of a match against flint, a hiss as she held the flame to the first wick.

While he'd done some more minor repairs to the barn, she'd cooked some packaged pasta and heated a jar of spaghetti sauce.

"Dinner is served," she said, laughter in her voice. "It's not much, but at least we won't starve."

Laughter? Susan had never laughed at herself.

He joined Meghan at the table, piling a mound of rigatoni in the middle of his plate and drowning it with sauce.

"Are you okay?" she asked, a forkful of rigatoni speared and held near her mouth...the mouth he recalled tasting. "You're quiet."

"Fine," he lied, realizing he'd rarely felt less fine. He felt as though he was on the outside of a store, a thick glass window separating him from touching, holding, caressing. The very things he wanted most.

Kyle realized he didn't want to vanish from her life as if he'd never existed, as if their time together never existed. He wanted to leave her with something to remember— other than the obvious.

After dinner, Meghan turned on water for his hot chocolate and her tea.

While she stood at the stove, the perfect starting point for her holiday-to-remember came to his mind. "Any plans for dessert?" he asked.

She turned to face him, hips resting against a cupboard as she waited for the kettle to boil. "I think I have a box of cheesecake mix in the pantry. Is the milk still good?"

"Meghan?"

"Hmm?" She adjusted the kettle on the burner.

"Do you make anything besides bread from scratch?"

"Yep." The boiling water whistled. She turned off the stove. "Tea."

He grinned.

"Hope you'll still respect me in the morning, but I have a terrible confession," she said in hushed tones.

He inclined his head.

"Tonight was about the extent of my culinary talents. Well, that and the stew we had last night. Of course, that doesn't really count since I started it from a container. Just add a few frozen veggies and pretend the canned ones aren't really in there."

She definitely needed someone to care for her.

Kyle stoically ignored the nagging inner voice that insisted *he* could be that man.

"Wait," she added. "I also make pancakes. They're one of my weaknesses. Drowned in syrup and powdered sugar."

"I can feel my arteries clogging."

She smiled. "Talking about it is nothing compared to actually eating them, so I restrict myself to every other Sunday."

"Can you make cookies?"

"Cookies?"

"You know, the things you dunk in milk." He paused, timing the remainder of his sentence, and said, "And leave out for Santa."

Her expression clouded.

"Don't tell me, you never left cookies for Santa."

"I did." She blinked several times in quick succession. "Once."

He winced. Her eyes momentarily shuttered shut. Not for anything did he want her reliving that kind of pain. Yet he hoped the memories he intended to leave behind would replace some of the bitterness. "My grandma used to make Christmas cookies," he said, plowing ahead. "Shouldn't be too difficult to figure it out." He hoped.

Obviously ignoring him, she stood, picked up her plate and, with squared shoulders, walked to the sink.

He drummed his fingers on the table, considering his options. Decision made, he rapped his knuckles on the wood, then stood. In a few steps, she stood within reach of his arms.

She belonged in them, near him, with him.

He tamped down the wayward, renegade thoughts. He always managed to control his emotions; Kyle told himself Meghan wouldn't shake him of that. "If you want to do the dishes, I'll head out to the barn and get the eggs and butter. Maybe we can make the cookies look like trees, or bells." He shrugged. "Something festive."

She whirled, brows tightly drawn, fists clenched at her side. "Drop it."

"Drop what?"

"All this talk about Christmas. Please. Let it go."

Their camaraderie vanished, exposing her hurt. He took another step toward her, she held up her hands, still tightly balled. Her breasts pressed against the sweater as she forced sharp breaths from deep inside. He'd sparked her passion. Just as he wanted. He reached for her shoulders. "Meghan—"

She shrugged him off. "Darn it, Kyle, I don't do Christmas. I never have, never will." Looking him square in the eyes, she added, "Get over it."

"You get over it, Meghan. You're an adult. Grow up."

In the dim light, he saw her pale. Color drained from her face, leaving vulnerability etched in its place.

"Damn you," she whispered.

He strained to hear her, afraid he'd pushed too far. Yet he knew he'd gamble and push further if it meant he'd help her put her past behind her.

Her chin trembled, and he wondered if it was a sob that

caught in her voice when she said, "You don't have any idea what you're talking about."

"Christmas is for caring, and sharing. You have parents who are self-absorbed fools. That doesn't mean you should pretend an entire season doesn't exist."

"How dare you presume to tell me what I should feel, how I should act?" Sucking in a shallow breath, she rushed on. "You know nothing about me, nothing about how I think or feel. And you certainly don't have the right to tell me to celebrate a holiday that means nothing to me."

"Christmas is a chance to bring out the best in all of us."

"Is it? Is it really, Kyle? Then why did my husband serve me with divorce papers on Christmas Eve?"

Silence.

Loud, thunderous silence.

Then his ears filled with the sound of his own blood rushing.

Ex-husband.

Divorce papers on Christmas Eve.

He digested the information, cursing viciously, resenting the hell out of the unknown man for having known her, and worse, for having hurt her. She was a woman to be cherished, not destroyed. "Damn it."

He released a sigh, but not the energy that was suddenly pent up deep inside. "I'm sorry, Meghan."

"Maybe Christmas brings out the best in some people, but if so, I haven't had any experience with it." She looked up at him, directing all her honesty and pain toward him. "Jack and I were married in June. Mom and Dad insisted on paying for everything, even though they knew I was making a mistake by marrying so young. They had to keep up appearances. I had all the trappings from a fairy tale—a fabulous gown and real diamonds in my tiara, if you can imagine that."

She shook her head, and when she continued, her voice was low and haunted.

Coward that he was, Kyle suddenly wished he hadn't pushed her back against a figurative wall.

"Mom and Dad invited everyone they knew and pulled out all the stops—a church ceremony and a catered dinner that cost more money than I made last year.

"By Thanksgiving, things had started to fall apart, but I still believed, and I took my vows seriously. Besides, I wanted—needed—to prove my parents wrong."

She moved away a few feet, then wrapped her hands across her middle. Pain, that he'd inflicted, ghosted across her features.

"Not only that but I was looking forward to having a real Christmas."

"Your first *real* Christmas," Kyle added. A knot hardened in his gut, as though a punch had landed there and kept on punishing.

"I was tying the ribbon on his present when the papers arrived."

"Son of a bitch."

"Jack…" She looked at Kyle, not trying to disguise the torment she'd experienced. "Jack spent the holiday with his pregnant girlfriend."

Kyle raked spread fingers into his hair, frowning when he dragged across the knot on his scalp.

She dropped her hands to her side. "Please, don't give me meaningless platitudes about December 25. There's nothing special about it, nothing extraordinary that makes people behave better or different. It's just another day. And if I could skip it, I would."

Quietly, determinedly, he challenged, "So it's not just another day."

Her eyes narrowed and hazel sparked with golden daggers. Her voice trembled, thick with emotion. "What do you want from me, my heart served on a platter for your picking? Fine. Here it is, Kyle, in honest to goodness color. Every memory of Christmas is an aching gape in my heart, filled with pain. Every time I try to take a remembrance out and examine it, with the supposed understanding of adulthood and distance of years, I still cry.

"Each year I see wreaths and bows, trees and stars, lights and tinsel and ornaments. And I don't have a single pleasant point of reference. Presents aren't for me. And I don't really have a family to get together with. On the radio, there's lots of carols, but I don't smile.

"There's one that sifts through my mind, though, and plays over and over. Silent Night."

He nodded. "I love that carol."

"Well, it's symbolic of my life. Every one of my Christmases has been a silent night." She batted away a tear that seeped onto her eyelashes.

In trying to help, he'd made things worse. He probed that thought, and it stung. God only knew what he'd done to her.

Then she lashed out at him, firing another lethal arrow. "But at least I have the courage to face my fears, instead of running away from them."

"Do you Meghan?" he asked silkily. "Then why are you hiding out?"

She paled, and he nearly relented. But it was easy to fire arrows and not as easy to dodge them. Continuing, he asked, "What have you done that's so different than what I did?"

She blinked, hurt etched on her face. What right did he have to presume to try and change her life? Memories weren't something that could be deliberately made.

"You're right," she admitted softly. She sucked her lower lip between her teeth. "I'm sorry."

"I deserved it."

"No." She shook her head. "You didn't."

She returned to him and the tension inside him thickened tenfold. Rising onto her toes, she stroked her fingers down the curve of his jaw. He shivered involuntary, the drag of her touch oddly intimate.

Want, a feeling he was learning to equate with her touch, spiked. He captured her hand and moved it away.

"I don't know what it is about you," she said. "That makes me act this way."

He was aware of the way the curve of her knuckles snuggled into the fit of his palm.

"I'm usually even tempered."

He raised his brows.

"Usually," she added, nodding, as if that would make him believe her. "And I'm never rude...well, usually never rude."

"Usually."

"Usually," she repeated. A hint of a smile formed, then disappeared before completely taking hold. "But when you're around..." Meghan trailed off, then broke the contact of their gazes.

Lamplight flickered, playing on the silken highlights in her hair. He wanted nothing more than to tangle his hands in the strands as she surrendered to him.

"When you're around," she said again, "rational thought is all but impossible."

It was an admission of sorts...a beginning.

"You make me react, make me feel things I shouldn't."

He placed his thumb beneath her chin and exerted gentle pressure, tipping back her head. "Who says you shouldn't feel them?"

"Me." She blinked. "Common sense."

"What do you feel, Meghan?"

For several long seconds, she didn't answer. "Kyle..."

He remained silent.

And so did she.

"What do you feel?" he asked again, hoping to shatter the wall she was trying to build.

"Passion," she confessed.

The blurted admission sucked air from his lungs. When she continued, he struggled to think straight.

"It's something...something that seems totally beyond my control."

"And you don't like feeling out of control."

"No, I don't." She wiggled away from him, disappearing back toward the table. Sipping from her wine, she regarded him over the rim.

He called on the patience he'd cultivated in many years of boardroom evasions. She was on the run, that meant he bothered her more than she cared to admit. Hell, she bothered him. More than *he* cared to admit.

She sipped again.

He waited, wondering if she was stalling. Kyle refused to shatter the quiet, though, and speak first.

"Passion is a funny thing." She sat, swirling the long crystal stem between her thumb and forefinger.

A candle flickered near her, casting her in secretive shadows. He wanted to peel each of those secrets away, leaving her as open and exposed as he felt.

"I felt it, strongly, for Jack," she said, her voice hardly audible. "It flared quickly."

Still, he resisted moving closer. She seemed to need distance, and difficult as it was, he'd give it to her.

"But it burned itself out every bit as quickly."

"Meghan..." He didn't finish, not knowing exactly what to say.

"It was a long time ago," she continued after taking a delicate sip of her wine.

Hungrily he watched her, noting all her subtle nuances.

"Marriage and divorce made me stronger. I don't know

if I would have ever started making angels or bought this house if he hadn't left me."

He forced his gaze away from her mouth. "And what about your heart?"

She shifted, apparently avoiding his question. She tucked one leg beneath her, swung the other back and forth in small arcs. "I don't know. I don't think I'm afraid of love...."

"But?" he prompted when she trailed off, apparently into the past.

She finally met his gaze as she said, "But I don't trust it. My parents had passion, for everything except me, their only child. Jack had passion for anything in a skirt."

"All men aren't like that."

"No?"

"No. Some men take their commitments seriously, take their obligations to heart."

"Like you?"

"Yeah." He thought of the future ahead of him, his reluctance to walk that path. And yet he was determined to do what was right, no matter the cost to himself. "Like me."

Kyle glanced at the serene angel sitting on the countertop, as if he could draw inspiration of sorts from the piece of sculptured clay. Then he joined Meghan at the table, picking up his own wine and taking a deep drink. "Meghan, I have a proposition."

Gold spiked again in her eyes. Lord, he loved that uncontrolled change, reflecting her inner soul, despite her attempts to act cool and composed.

"Let me give you new memories," he said. He slid the base of his glass onto the table, reached for her hand and covered it. "We're stuck with each other for the time being."

Her leg stopped swinging.

"We might as well make the best of it," he added. "New memories that when you take them out and examine them, make you smile."

"Kyle," she said, "memories can't be deliberately made."

She leaned back, almost as if she was distancing herself. The fact she'd voiced his own misgivings didn't deter him. He'd carved out a path of determination—nothing would sway him from his course. "Can't they?"

Meghan allowed her head to tip back, revealing the length of the slender column of her neck. He ached to trail a thumb down sensitive skin, feel the throb of her pulse with his tongue, teach her to trust passion along with Christmas.

Kyle adjusted the waistband of his jeans.

Looking at her, he focused on her past, his desire to give her something for the future. "A chance, Meghan, that's all I'm asking for.

"Can you do that, for me? For yourself?"

She was quiet for so long, he worried that he'd blown it so badly that he wouldn't have an opportunity to save it.

"Cookies?" she asked softly, several long seconds later as she brought her head back into position.

He heard the hesitation in her tone and read the verge of capitulation in her whiskey-colored eyes. Telling himself to tread carefully, as if signing a multimillion-dollar deal.

Instantly he scratched that thought.

Meghan was more important than any multimillion-dollar deal he'd ever signed. And the stakes were higher. "Winter cookies," he said.

Lightly, she outlined her upper lip with the tip of her tongue. A surge of unprepared-for desire walloped him. One thing was for damn sure, he realized. Alcohol hadn't dulled a single one of his senses.

Not one bit.

She slowly nodded.

"Meghan?"

She lifted her gaze to meet his.

"Come here."

He stood; their eyes locked. He recalled the anguish of her words, the pain in her voice. He'd uncovered the pain, and knew the next step, that of unwrapping the passion that spiraled her out of control, was every bit as important....

Eight

The line between common sense and want blurred.

On wobbly legs, she crossed to him.

Her heart thundered...his eyes emanated the corresponding lightning. She'd opened her heart, and although she doubted he could wish away her pain and replace it with something better, she was helpless to resist.

After all, she'd already been hurt. Kyle couldn't cause any more damage than she'd already sustained.

His eyes seemed to spark, the illusion heightened by the jumping flame of the candle's wick. She knew his intent and surrendered, anyway, to the promise she knew he couldn't keep.

Their lips met; she drew in his scent, inhaling the healthiness of hard work, the crispness of the mountain air.

His kiss tasted of his promise, lasting a long, long time. She caught the tantalizing overtone of hope. A corresponding healing began in the private place she hadn't probed in years, not since she'd calculatedly closed it off.

But with Kyle…

His tongue danced with hers, a slow, enticing waltz. She swayed forward, allowing him to support her weight. Reaching up, she tangled her fingers in his hair, holding on when the tempo changed.

Kyle's pelvis pressed against her in timing with his more sensual assault. Enticing gave way to erotic. He deepened the kiss, his hands sliding down her spine. With his palm on her behind, he nudged her closer.

Her nipples tightened into knots, and she felt warmth flow through her, becoming a needy tingling.

Meghan closed her eyes, listening to their sounds, reveling in the power of desire and fulfillment.

She felt him, hard against soft. She felt her own, all-too-real response, yielding and simultaneously wanting. She felt out of control, couldn't think of how to stop it, realized she didn't want to stop it.

"Me-ghan…" He broke her name into two pieces, then eased them together again in a sensual whisper. "Meghan."

She opened her eyes, blinked a couple of times and realized his gaze was firmly fixed on her features. He moved his hands, bringing them up to curl around her shoulders, his fingers carving into her with the same urgency his eyes communicated.

"Tell me to stop, Meghan."

She should seize his offer, halting the insanity before it started. But it had been so long. Emotional hunger drove her, urging her. While she'd already recognized the fact he probably couldn't cover the previously inflicted scars, he could give her something to remember in the long months that separated winter from spring.

Maybe, just maybe, the nights wouldn't seem so long or the days so empty. "I can't tell you to stop, Kyle." From deep inside, she searched for a serving of courage. "I don't want you to stop."

His eyelids dropped slightly, desire darkening the tumultuous blue of his eyes.

In a single move, he swooped her from the floor, cradling her in his arms. Myriad thoughts sashayed through her as he carried her into the living room.

She snuggled against his chest, hearing the hurried thump of his heart. In his protection she felt safe. Secure. Wanted. Special.

Kyle gently placed her on the couch, then added a couple of pieces of wood to the fire. After poking and arranging them so that flames of warmth flicked at the pine, he adjusted the grate.

"Candles?" he asked. "Or just firelight?"

She battled a sudden case of nerves. "Firelight."

Kyle picked up the stack of folded linens from the small end table. She stood, fingers trembling, and took one end of the sheet.

"Let's move it closer to the fire," he said. "I don't want you to get cold."

The image of being naked before him, exposed and at her most vulnerable, sent a chill careering through her. Ordering herself to be brave, she crouched to spread the cotton across the carpet. Meghan smoothed the edges, then adjusted them again.

Aware of Kyle watching her, she glanced up, releasing her hold on the sheet. He didn't wear the smile she expected, rather his features contained a tenderness that threatened to unravel her.

He offered his palm, she slid hers on top, then felt a rush of warmth as he closed his fingers around her hand. He helped her up. No sounds, except those of a crackling fire and her shuddering pulse disturbed the intimacy.

"Don't be nervous," he said.

Her attempted grin faltered. "Easy for you to say."

"We'll take it as slow as you like."

He maintained his hold on her hand, as if afraid she might run. She wouldn't. As scared as she was, she wanted this, wanted him.

"We've got all night."

With his free hand, Kyle feathered her hair from her forehead, then traced his thumbnail across her eyebrows. Her lips parted slowly, and a soft sigh escaped. He trailed lower, outlining her bottom lip a single time, then again. Seemingly of its own volition, her tongue sneaked forward. Kyle rested his fingertip on her tongue, and she gently closed her mouth.

He drew in a sharp breath, and a feeling of heady knowledge sneaked through her. She possessed the same power to affect him as much as he affected her. Testing the bounds, she curled her tongue around him, sucking his fingertip deeper into her mouth.

Kyle's brows arced together.

When she finally released her hold, he continued his lazy, downward exploration. Cradling her chin, he stroked one side of her jaw with his thumb, the other with his fingers.

A sensation, akin to the beginnings of a fire like the one he'd lit earlier, began to stoke. Bit by bit, she became more sensually aware.

Her head tipped back as he continued his tactile exploration. She knew where this would lead, and savored each second as he brought each part of her to life.

His fingers moved down the column of her neck.

"I've been wanting to do this," he said.

Meghan had dreamed, too.

She shivered as his mouth replaced his fingers. Warmth seeped in when he hovered over her pulse point. Her heartbeat increased, its rhythm fast and undeniably sexual. When he actually touched the tip of his tongue against her skin, her knees started to buckle.

As always, he was there, to protect, to save. Fluidly he maneuvered them both to their knees.

Kyle paused before capturing the bottom of her sweater and pulling it up.

Under his appraisal, she experienced no embarrassment. How could she, when he acted as though she were precious? Ever since she'd been old enough to know the difference, *this* was the fairy-tale way she'd imagined being treated.

Her breasts felt full and heavy, throbbing as he swept his gaze down. This time, he placed his hands on her ribs and stroked his thumbs up, following her rib cage. He skipped over the clasp holding her bra together, then outlined the lacy cups.

She groaned, wanting.

He snagged the bra straps and reverently lifted them from her shoulders. Instinctively she arched forward, the material barely covering her. "Kyle..."

The urgency in her tone must have communicated to him, for he returned to the fastener, flicking it open. Her breasts spilled into his palms, nipples thrusting forward to demand his caress.

Kyle complied.

His thumbnails dragged across the tips of her breasts and breath whooshed from her. Between her thighs, she throbbed and ached. He cupped her breasts, and she reached for him, locking her hands behind his neck. Gently, he squeezed her nipples between his thumb and forefinger. She called out his name. When he bestowed a kiss, followed by a nip to each, she knew she wobbled on the edge.

Too many clothes barred him from her. Urgency raced through her blood.

Obviously sensing the change of tempo within her, Kyle met her eyes. "Meghan?"

She could barely think, struggling to find words in a mind fogged by the reactions his touch had caused. "Make...make love to me."

He smiled.

Meghan fumbled with the buttons on his shirt. "Darn it," she muttered when one refused to give.

He chuckled, the sound rich and inviting. As she neared the bottom, she noticed the tails were still tucked into the waistband of his jeans.

Fingers shaking, she tugged, managed the last button, then pulled apart the sides. She inhaled slowly, trying to control the very feelings that zinged out of control.

Despite the internal frenzy, she couldn't hurry through this.

She flattened her palms against his bare chest, then slowly explored the texture of him. When she unintentionally moved over one of his nipples, he hissed in a breath.

Emboldened, she flicked the tip of her thumbnail across again. Then she repeated the caress on the other side. Kyle hooked her wrist in his hand.

"Fair's fair," she whispered.

"Not if you want this over in less than two minutes."

She smiled, feeling, for the first time ever, the headiness of control. Recklessly she disregarded his warning, seeking out, with her mouth, the same response he'd coaxed from her.

He leaned back, she followed.

With her teeth, she gently abraded. He groaned.

"Enough."

But it wasn't, not for her, not nearly enough.

She looked up, that insistent demand inside returning again. Its complement radiated from his eyes. She wanted completion, so did he.

"Stand up," he said softly.

She gulped. Although she'd been married, Jack hadn't taken time to teach her, to encourage her, to truly love her.

"Trust me," Kyle asked. "I won't ask you to do anything you're not ready for."

Using the hand he offered as support, she stood. Still on his knees, Kyle wrapped his arms around her, holding her steady as he placed his lips to her, just below her ribs. She reached for his shoulders but found nothing other than air. Not surprisingly, though, he increased the pressure of his hold, giving the support she so desperately needed.

When he kissed her again, she thought she was prepared. Yet her lower body still threatened to give out.

"Meghan, I'm going to finish undressing you."

She nodded after trying, and failing, to form words. Her hands tangled in his hair when his hands eased between the elastic at the waist of her leggings and bare skin.

After he eased them down, she stepped from them, separated from him only by the thin material of satin panties.

His inhalation was knife sharp; his soft words male and earthy.

The moisture between her legs was just as real. She shuddered, wondering if he knew the extent of her reaction to his nearness and his assault on her sensitive nerves.

Motions deliberate, he pushed the satin panties down, over her hips, her thighs, then finally, completely off.

Cool air danced across her skin, only to be replaced by his heat from his hand.

He wended upward, on the inside of her legs, brushing close, but not nearly close enough to her most sensitive spot.

"Meghan, I'll take care of you."

She knew he would.

"Do you trust me?"

"Yes," she whispered.

He stood. Holding on to her shoulder, he used the toe of his right boot to dislodge the left, then leaned over to remove the second.

She shyly reached for the snap at the top of his jeans. Unable to loosen it, she cast a pleading glance toward him. With unspoken accord, he helped.

Then, instead of unzipping himself, Kyle held her hand in place. A new flush flirted with her face when she took hold of the zipper's tab. He strained against the denim, and she gulped, understanding he was as ready as she.

Each moment, fewer trappings existed to keep them apart.

"Finish undressing me," he said.

She nodded, pushing away her hesitation to become the lover he dared her to be. Oddly, her participation made her more aware of her femininity...never had she felt more sexy. Womanly.

Tooth by tooth, the zipper parted, a click of metal for each tug. As she crouched to lower the denim, she wildly wondered how the material had ever accommodated him.

Looking up, she lowered his briefs, then gulped a shallow breath.

Her stomach fluttered. For an incredibly tense moment she wondered how they would ever fit together.

He joined her on the sheet, capturing her lips for a kiss that banished all thoughts except for the one that said they were meant to be together.

After he dragged a pillow from the couch, she lay back. He propped his head on his elbow, watching her, cataloging emotions she couldn't hide. Beneath his lazy exploration, hesitation faded. Passion began to build again. He reignited her response with his touch, his taste.

After unhurriedly stroking, he moved, cupping his hand between her thighs. She arched against him when he lighted across the sensitive spot hidden from view and cried out, "Kyle!"

Reckless yearning made her clutch at him. "I can't... I want..."

He was driving her insane. It was too much and not enough, all at the same time.

Kyle paused, reaching for his leather saddlebag. He dragged it onto the floor, fought the zipper, ending up dumping the entire contents. He sought out his wallet and removed several packages from one of the compartments. "God, I hope these are still good," he muttered.

The fact he didn't often have use for them thrilled her. And that he'd thought of all the angles—especially when she'd been too swept away to think at all—endeared him to her. He was a man who could be trusted.

A man who kept his promises. A man who'd be there if he said he would.

He ripped open a packet, and in a few seconds, she felt the insistence of his arousal against her. Her pulse surged within her, and she raised her hips, seeking him.

Kyle slowly sank into her. She moaned at the slowness of his possession, even as she knew she needed the time for her body to accommodate his penetration.

She met his eyes, noted the sheen of dampness on his forehead. "Take me," she whispered, then the breath rushed from her as he did.

He filled her completely. Meghan reached to hold his shoulders, realizing she'd never felt so whole before.

He began to move, his strokes deep and hard. Her eyes closed as emotion collided with reason, and both faded beneath Kyle's touch.

Insistently, intensity built, driving her to the edge. Kyle placed his hands beneath her hips, raising her slightly, making the feelings so much more unbelievable.

Colors and sensations swirled in her mind, and she cried

out his name. Seconds later, those sensations overtook her as he drove deep a final time. She slid over the edge, clutching him.

He stopped for a few moments as the wash of excitement receded.

"You okay?" he asked.

She opened her eyelids and smiled up at him, seeing the tension that still painted the small area between his knitted eyebrows. "Fine," she whispered, the word emerging hoarse.

Slowly, as she became aware of her surroundings again, she realized he hadn't found the same satisfaction as she had. "Kyle?"

Obviously no more needed to be said.

He placed a gentle kiss on the tip of her nose, then began to move again. She met each move, this time keeping her eyes open to see his reactions.

His frown deepened, lips tightened, jaw tensed. She wrapped her arms around him, raising herself when he pushed. He groaned and thrust hard, and she was aware of the throb that seemed to echo through her.

They were one, for this time.

And she sighed, unable, for that particular moment, to think of anything she'd like more.

Lexie descended from heaven and plucked the furry feline from the third-story ledge. Then she sighed in relief. She'd saved the sorry rascal. Again.

The kitten didn't approve of the fact its quest for a sparrow had been interrupted, and it looked up, baring its sharp teeth. With a hiss, the calico cat, Curiosity, raked sharp claws down Lexie's white silken robe.

Scowling at the maniacal feline, she set it on the tile floor—on the opposite side of the room from the food dish. She had averted crisis, not that the beastly little animal appreciated her efforts at all. In relief Lexie glided upward, back to Grandma Aggie.

"Michael certainly gave you a formidable task," Grandma Aggie said sympathetically.

"I didn't like cats when I was alive. I don't like them any better now. I was dreading puppy duty, but this is worse, much worse."

"Michael was just trying to give you something to do to keep you out of trouble."

"It didn't work." Lexie grinned. "I just have to work overtime, but the rewards are worth it." She glanced down at her charge, snuggled beneath a blanket, hair fanned across Kyle's chest.

"I had my back turned," Grandma Aggie said in response to the unasked question.

Lexie allowed a sigh of satisfaction. She'd saved the kitten, and it looked as though the humans were well on their way to working out their problems. Soon, she hoped, there would be a marriage, followed by an infant to watch over.

The way Meghan had responded to Kyle's charms, that looked like an imminent possibility.

A Christmas miracle. Surely, if she—and Aggie, of course—pulled off the feat, Michael would relent and give some other heavenly inhabitant responsibility for Curiosity the cat. Surely…

"It looks promising," Lexie said, voicing her internal thoughts as Kyle smoothed a hand through Meghan's hair.

Grandma Aggie frowned. "He's still planning to go home."

Lexie's eyes opened wide. "Still?"

"We knew Kyle's a man who takes his responsibilities seriously; that's his greatest strength as well as his biggest weakness."

"Surely, now…?"

Aggie shook her head, and her halo flashed in the golden glow.

Lexie thought fast. There had to be something, anything she could do. If Meghan only ended up hurt worse than she already had been, Lexie's troubles had barely begun.

Well…it simply didn't bear thinking about.

"Cookies?" Meghan repeated Kyle's suggestion sleepily.

Her voice contained the husk of sex, and it shot a wild fire through him.

"You still want to make cookies?" she repeated.

"I seem to have worked up an appetite," Kyle said.

She smiled, and his heart seemed to turn over. Immediately he dismissed that thought as ridiculous. A heart couldn't really turn over.

Or could it?

She wiggled her breast against his side. He reached for her, feeling the nipple swell against his hand. He didn't remember anything so erotic before. It made him want. Again.

Once hadn't been enough. Not even close.

Her small whimper caused his gut to tighten.

As if in response, a thunderous crash ricocheted from the kitchen into the living room. Meghan jumped. Instinctively, Kyle drew her closer.

"Looks like you're not the only one thinking of his stomach," Meghan teased.

A second crash followed, and Snowflake barked pitifully. Kyle swore as he reached for his jeans.

"A can probably landed on his paw," Meghan said.

"I'll check it out." He stood, shoving reluctant legs into the jeans, then looked down at Meghan.

Blond layers of her hair hung in riotous disarray, framing her face and encouraging him to explore the thick texture.

The blanket covered her breasts but left her shoulders alluringly bare. Her eyes, Lord, her eyes. Their hazel depths seemed to sparkle in the fire's light, framing an invitation to hurry back.

He nearly forgot about the mutt.

Snowflake hadn't forgotten, though. Kyle heard the dog knock over the bag of kibbles, followed by a telltale ripping. "Can he sleep outside?"

She smiled, that same seductive curl to her lips that encouraged him to remember the tempting taste of her mouth. With great reluctance, he grabbed a flashlight and went after Snowflake.

When Kyle directed the beam of light at the dog, Snowflake stopped chomping and looked up. He whined, as if saying he was sorry, but he hadn't wanted to wait any longer. "I know," Kyle said. He ruffled the dog's fur and scooped a pile of food into the metal bowl before cleaning up the spilled nuggets.

"Were you serious about cookies?"

Turning, Kyle looked at Meghan. He hadn't heard her approach but was glad to see her. She wore her robe, belted across the waist. Tonight's vision of her in the cotton was worse than last night's had been. Last night, all he had was his imagination. Tonight, he knew what lay beneath.

He was hungry, all right, but not necessarily for food.

Kyle reminded himself of his promise to leave her with memories of Christmas. And it was a good bet her ex-husband hadn't made cookies with her.

"Yeah," he said. "I was serious."

She nodded. "I'm game."

"I'll get the eggs and butter from the cooler in the barn."

Wrapping her arms around her middle, Meghan glanced toward the window and asked, "Isn't it too cold to go outside?"

"Promise to warm me up when I come back in?"

Her eyelids opened wide, then dropped slightly, shading her eyes in an unconsciously sensual way. She didn't have an ounce of artifice anywhere, he was sure of it, and that made her that much more beautiful.

Before he changed his mind and carried her back to their makeshift bed, he quickly kissed her.

Less than five minutes later, he returned, exposed fingers chilled.

She'd lit a couple of lanterns and taken several bowls from the cupboard, along with measuring spoons and cups. The scene looked so...there was that word again: *domestic.*

And appealing.

Shoving away the intrusion, he placed the ingredients onto the counter. Kyle took off his jacket, and she reached for it, hanging it next to hers. What would it be like, he wondered, to find her waiting for him at the end of a long day?

"You're cold." She took his hands in hers. Then she rose onto the balls of her feet, offering a kiss.

He took it.

She'd promised to warm him up. Cold became a distant memory, tomorrow a reality he didn't want to face.

"Cookies," she reminded him.

"Yeah. Right." He swallowed. "Do you have a cookbook?"

Her eyes narrowed in suspicion. "I thought you said you knew how to make them."

"I lied."

"You...lied?"

"I want to give you memories, Meghan. To replace the ones that hurt you."

Her lips parted, giving him a teasing look at her tongue.

"I...never thought I'd approve of someone lying to me."

He held up a hand in surrender.

"Okay, Kyle," she said. "Let's make new memories.

"I think I still have a cookbook I got for a wedding present." She searched a shelf. "Betty Crocker," she said triumphantly, taking out the hardback book still wrapped in its protective packaging.

She tossed the plastic shrink wrap at the trash can. She missed, as usual.

"Want to bring the flashlight here?"

Kyle complied, after scooping up the trash and depositing it in the can. He stood behind her, close, very close, and directed the beam over her shoulder.

He nuzzled her neck and she shifted. He moved forward, her buttocks pressing against him.

He hardened.

"Hold the light steady," she said.

"Then keep still," he ordered.

"I can't when you're doing that."

"What?" He allowed his teeth to abrade the sensitive area of her neck, then laved the hurt with his mouth. He did it again, moving lower. She tipped her head to the side with a little sigh, granting him access to her shoulder.

"That," she gasped, pushing back against him.

Making cookies, he realized, wasn't going to be a thing like he remembered, either.

Snowflake turned over his bowl, then sat down, head tilted to one side.

"We need...need to turn on the..."

"Oh, I am," he said.

She moved again, whispering Kyle's name.

He was close, closer than he'd ever been outside a bed. What was it about her? He always possessed iron-willed control. Or had, until Meghan.

Realizing they'd soon be doing it in the kitchen, he backed off a couple of inches, redirecting the light at the cookbook. "Let's make the damn cookies," he said, "so I can take you back to bed."

"I thought you were hungry."

"I am." Their gazes locked.

"Oh."

Her smile was secretive. Seductive. And he was tempted to try to unravel its meanings.

"Then we'd better make those cookies," she said, "so we can satisfy both appetites."

"Meghan?"

"Hmm?"

"Read the recipe."

She did. Kyle fought for concentration as he looked for the flour and sugar.

"Bottom shelf," she said.

He was staring at the bottom shelf and couldn't see it. All he saw were visions of blond hair wrapped around his fingers, the way her brows had drawn together as she cried out his name when her climax overtook her.

Meghan crouched near him, gave a purely female type of sigh and said, "There's the flour. The sugar's next to it."

"You think men can't find things."

"Can they?" she asked. "My dad never could. You—"

"Can't, either," he said, finishing for her. Placing his hands on her ribs, he pulled her up. "I was distracted."

"Distracted?" Her voice was hardly above a squeak.

"By thoughts of you."

"Me?"

"The way you bit my shoulder."

"Did not," she insisted breathlessly.

"The way you arched your hips against mine."

Meghan shook her head.

"And the way I still want to taste you." He purposefully allowed his gaze to travel lower, stopping below her waist. Then he met her eyes again. "All of you."

The breath she'd been taking rushed out through her open mouth. He grinned. "Now, you find the baking soda."

It was a dangerous game they were playing, he knew. No rules. Which suited him fine. Making up rules as he went was a specialty.

A minute or so later, he added, "It's on the top shelf."

He turned on the oven and cracked the eggs while she thumped the baking soda against the counter's edge. Kyle refrained from saying anything, then began whistling a Christmas song.

"I'll jingle your bells," she murmured, the words a seductive purr.

He stopped whistling.

She measured powdered sugar and butter into the bowl, along with vanilla extract. "I need the eggs," she said.

"Allow me." Time to turn the tables. Again, he moved behind her. After pouring the eggs into the mixture, he reached around her to place his hand over hers on the wooden mixing spoon.

Together they stirred, his upper arm brushing her breast with each long stroke. He wondered if the nipple was lengthening, if her breasts felt heavy and full.

Their circular motions became slower and slower as they stirred. He noticed the change in her breathing, normal being replaced by shallow.

His own followed suit.

As they started back around, he nipped the top of her ear. Simultaneously he moved forward to catch her weight. Her shoulders rested against his chest before she moved away slightly.

"Flour," she said, the word lodging in her throat.

As for him, he didn't even try to speak.

Kyle dumped in unmeasured flour—it had worked for Grandma—then poured in some baking soda, taking the time to touch Meghan.

Flour flew as they resumed stirring, falling like the Colorado snow onto the counter.

The lapels of her robe parted, only a fraction of an inch, but the sight of silken skin was a reminder, sensually and physically.

Suddenly he wasn't paying a bit of attention to the dough, and plenty to the reaction of her body.

He took his hand off hers, trailing his knuckles down her throat, then unable to resist, inside her robe.

Her motions stilled. The spoon clattered.

"Kyle?"

Pausing, he turned her to face him. "Yeah?"

"The dough has to chill for two hours."

"Thank God."

Nine

The fireplace snapped and crackled.

Driven by desire and fed by urgency, he fumbled with the tight knot cinching her robe closed.

Her fingers found the snap at his waist. Her fingernails scraped his skin and he sucked in a breath.

"Sorry."

He didn't respond. Instead, he concentrated on undressing her. She moved his fingers aside and untied the belt. With his palms, he slid the robe from her shoulders. The fabric pooled around her feet, leaving her before him, naked.

Need, raw and stark, claimed him.

Within seconds, he'd removed his jeans.

Kyle left her only long enough to fit the protective sheath in place. He entered her in a single thrust, burying himself.

She cried out, dragging him closer.

Their motions were well timed, two halves of a more perfect whole.

For Kyle, this was more than sex, deeper even than love-making. It transcended everything he'd ever known. But her physical response wasn't enough, he wanted more—wanted her heart.

Their mouths joined, tongues mating.

Kyle gritted his teeth as he fought to hold off his pleasure until he'd first assured her satisfaction. Sweat beaded his brow and slicked where their skin met.

He balanced the majority of his weight on his elbows, trying not to crush her.

"Kyle!"

She dragged him on top of her. The threads of his remaining control fractured as he found his release.

Seconds later—or maybe it was minutes later—the sound of blood thundering in his ears receded. He managed to regulate his breathing, but bringing his pulse back to normal was impossible.

"Quick" wasn't his usual style. Yet as he looked at the smile on Meghan's face, he didn't experience any regret.

He moved, lying on his side. The first rush of passion abated, he took the time to make a lazy exploration of her body.

He started with her hair, indulging in the fantasy of trailing his fingers through the various lengths and allowing the thick strands to spill through his open fingers.

Then he moved lower, outlining the brows that softly framed her eyes.

"Kyle?"

"Indulge me."

She nodded, the fireplace popped, and he continued, "I want to know you, Meghan, learn what triggers your response, discover what appeases it."

"I think..." She blinked, then her eyes closed completely.

"You think?" he prompted.

"You already have."

He chuckled with male triumph, then added, "I'm sure there's more." He outlined her mouth with his thumbnail. When her lips parted, he snuck inside. Gently she closed her teeth. Want, razor sharp, seemed to shoot through him, landing in his gut.

It wasn't possible to have this strong a reaction so soon. At least that's what Kyle told himself.

When she released him, he trailed his fingers down the column of her neck. Lazily he explored one of her breasts, tenderly cradling the weight in his palm.

He looked at her, noticed her eyes were now open wide and spiked with gold. Her honest acknowledgment of her physical pleasure fueled him, making him want to give more, leave her changed by their relationship...just as he felt changed.

Kyle then returned his attention to her nipple, noting the contrasting duskiness of the aureola against creamy white. He teased, flicking across the swollen tip, watching, fascinated by the subtle changes in height and hardness.

She squirmed under his attention, her hips rising from the sheet. He inhaled the faint musky scent of their love-making, caught the faint traces of a cologne she'd splashed on after her earlier shower.

Positioning himself in the cradle of her thighs, he suckled her breast, pulling a nipple into his mouth, adoring it with his tongue.

"I..."

He paused, waiting. "Tell me," he urged softly. "Tell me what you want, what you like."

She shook her head.

"This?" he asked, swirling around the distended tip.

"Y-yes."

He gave attention to her other breast, while closing his hand around the one he'd dampened. She was wriggling, her head tossing on the pillow. Parts of the sheet were knotted in her fists.

And when he shifted, wending downward, stroking between her thighs, she said again, "Yes."

His tongue found her cleft and she sank her heels into the floor, arching up. "More?" he asked, his breath warming her.

"No...I never...I don't..."

He spread her gently apart and felt her moistness, her readiness. She thrust her hips up, asking with her body. Kyle sought more from her, seeking to drive her inexorably to the edge.

Tenderly he again caressed with his tongue. She swore softly, but with a passion that encouraged him to intensify the pressure.

Her hands found his shoulders and her nails dug into him. How sweet the victory of trust tasted.

"Kyle, I..."

"Let go," he said softly. "Take what I'm offering."

Her breaths were labored, her buttocks tight, her response seductively female.

Gently he slipped a finger inside her, simulating their earlier lovemaking. Rhythmically she rocked beneath his touch.

Her shudder built, slowly, then faster and faster. Her hold on him dug deeper as her body sought more and more. He complied. He thrust into her. Her abdomen tightened. He applied slightly more pressure to the tiny nub, and she cried out.

As reality returned, he understood he'd promised her the gift of memories, but she'd selflessly given him more than he could ever offer her.

"Rolling pin?" She frowned. "I've never used one. Maybe in the drawer, under the stove."

While she separated the dough into two pieces, Kyle searched out the rolling pin. "Found it," he said, the statement sounding vaguely gloating.

"In that case, you must not be distracted enough." Meghan went to him, ignoring the feel of cold on her bare feet.

Being with Kyle, she didn't mind the inconvenience of the power cut, or the cold. Of course, she hadn't felt the cold much. If anything, she'd noticed the warmth. It amazed her that two people could generate so much heat. Rising onto her tiptoes, she laced her hands around his neck and kissed his lower lip.

He shoved the wooden utensil onto the countertop, letting her lead, but encouraging her with unspoken response. The awareness of her body was new, exciting, and she wanted to explore all the possibilities. Meghan had never seen herself as a sexual being before, but under Kyle's daring touch, she was learning.

And was anxious to continue the lessons.

She kissed him, deeply and for a long time. When he wrapped his arms around her, she released his neck, reaching instead for his back. She allowed one hand to slip down, until her palm met denim. His behind was firm and most definitely well shaped. "Nice tush," she whispered.

His eyes twinkled in the dancing lantern light.

"Yours, too," he said, turning to slip the words directly into her ear.

He nibbled her earlobe, sending a rush of warmth to her most intimate parts.

Kyle gathered a handful of her robe and pulled up the material from the back. His hand flattened against her naked flesh.

"Most definitely," Kyle said, "a nice tush."

His fingers teased between her legs, finding her heat and

causing her legs to weaken—to the point they could no longer hold her.

He'd turned the tables again, making her the student once more. She decided she liked being under his tutelage.

"We're going to starve," Meghan protested as he began to move against her, a tingle building.

"Let's starve."

She shivered when his eyes darkened. Drawing a lip between her teeth, she glanced at him. His pants were unsnapped, a V of hair disappearing downward. His small male nipples were aware, and his jeans were bulging.

Fingers trembling, she reached for the zipper. Kyle winced.

"That'll teach you to wear underwear."

"You're right." He swore, then adjusted the denim at the front.

He drew the zipper down the rest of the way, then kicked aside the small amount of clothes he'd worn.

"Be right back."

Meghan watched him, unconcernedly naked, admiring the leashed power of his masculine form.

For now, he was hers.

He returned to her, and using the wall to support her back and shoulders, Kyle lifted her.

"Like this?" she asked, an odd thrill finding her.

"If you're game?"

She smiled. Holding her hips firmly, he inched her down, slowly, slowly, filling her, stretching her.

She flexed her feet, seeking the security of the floor as he settled her on top of him.

"You okay?"

She didn't answer, unable to find words. She was more than okay, in fact, she felt wonderfully decadent and free.

"Meghan?"

Responding to the urgency in his voice, she met his gaze.

"I never imagined." She rested her hands on his shoulders. "Can we actually...?"

In answer, he simultaneously surged forward and up.

She gasped.

He was buried inside her, to the hilt. Her body accommodated him, and she felt him deep against her womb. If there was anything more wondrous, she couldn't name it.

Her head dropped forward as he drove inside her.

She cried out his name at the same time a desperate groan tore from him.

"What's that?" Meghan asked, scooting closer to stand next to Kyle. The shirt she wore—one of his—brushed her thighs, making her aware of their intimacy.

"That," he said, "is a tree."

"A tree?" She looked again, trying to see what he saw. "And the blob on top?"

"Is a star. All Christmas trees have stars on the top."

"Oh."

"Let's see your creations."

She frowned. "I don't have the hang of this Christmas thing yet."

"You've got a natural talent," he said. "I've seen your work."

"But I don't make angels out of cookie dough, especially cookie dough that's been rolled this many times."

Her breasts still tingled where his arms had continually brushed her. With him, making cookies was a sensual art. He stood behind her, hands covering hers on the pin, pushing forward—his maleness surging against her—then pulling back. And with slow, easy motions, they repeated the process.

It shocked her they'd gotten this far without heading back for their place near the crackling fire.

But she'd never imagined cooking could be like this.

Still, concentration was next to impossible with the zinging sexual tension that cloaked them.

No matter what they were doing, it led straight to one place...she couldn't get enough.

"Meghan?"

"Okay, okay." She took his hand and led him to the table, purposefully averting her gaze from the wall where he'd shown her another mystery, then helped her unravel it. "I told you, they're not much."

Her wreaths looked like doughnuts, which wasn't a surprise, since she'd used two glasses to cut the shapes. But the bells she'd cut freehand, with a knife.

"The bells are good. They actually look the way they're supposed to."

"Gee, thanks."

"I didn't mean it that way." He caught her chin between thumb and forefinger, gently turning her to look at him.

She grinned cheekily. "I know."

"You'll pay, Meghan."

"I hope so."

They slid the first batch in the oven, then each cut more cookies from the remaining dough. Kyle's stars were no better than his trees. And her snowmen looked already melted.

"Maybe they'll taste better than they look," she mused.

"Help me cut out this star," he said.

She left her final snowman—maybe she shouldn't have tried to give him a scarf—and went to help.

"Now I know why cookie cutters are big business," Kyle said.

"I think they were designed especially for us." She paused. The final word seemed to reverberate through the room. For a tantalizing moment, she considered the word, exploring the meanings.

Us.

The two of them. Together, to face the world along with the future. The house wouldn't feel so empty, she wouldn't be so lonely. Maybe there'd even be the pitter-patter of little footsteps to accompany a squeal of mischief.

Quickly though, she swallowed, ruthlessly shoving away the tempting images. She picked up the knife he'd been using, but instead of helping him with the shape, she cut the star herself.

Herself.

The single word served as a good reminder. She was by herself before he arrived, she'd be alone again when he left.

One thing was certain, though, he'd leave her with plenty of memories...just like he promised.

She only hoped they'd be enough to keep her company in the endless nights ahead.

Using a pot holder, she took the nonstick tray from the oven. While she readied the second batch for baking, Kyle pried beneath the cookies with a spatula. His star on top of his tree was the first casualty.

Kyle ate the evidence. "Not bad."

A crumb clung tenaciously to his lip, and she succumbed to the nagging voice that told her to wipe it away...with her tongue.

This time, they did end up near the fireplace. Kyle prodded the embers, then fed the hungry fire another log. Flames licked the wood, filling the air with the smoky scent of pine and adding the faint glow of intimacy.

He joined her, his lovemaking coaxing and unhurried...the antithesis of their last mating.

The cookies burned without either of them caring.

Meghan wrapped her arms around herself and pushed her chair away from her worktable. Tears blurred her vision, making it impossible to see the tiny features of the angel in front of her.

How could she have been so foolish?

Last night had been wonderful, terrific, unbelievable. And she'd made a huge mistake. Somewhere along the line, she'd allowed her emotions to tangle in the sensual exploration.

He'd given her memories, but in exchange, she'd foolishly offered her heart.

She knew better.

She knew better.

For nearly two weeks after Jack had served the divorce papers, she'd cried, become a recluse, nursing the callously inflicted wounds. Then one day, she'd contacted her own attorney, straightened her shoulders and made herself a solemn vow—not to love and, especially, not to trust again.

Meghan wiped the back of her hand across her eyes. Blinking rapidly, she tried to dissolve the tears she swore wouldn't fall.

She looked out the window, seeing a different landscape from the one that had been painted just yesterday.

The sun shone brightly, its rays toying with the snow, making it look like diamond dust had been casually scattered across the drifts. Deep blue skies dipped to meet distant mountains, craggy peaks proudly wearing white. A raven streaked across her vision to land atop a tree.

Trees.

They were everywhere, and each of them served as a reminder of the cookies they'd baked last night.

Winter cookies.

Christmas cookies.

She rested her forehead on the cold pane of glass, wishing desperately Kyle would leave today, taking with him his ridiculous ideas of Christmas.

She'd learned her lessons in the most painful way possible—through disillusionment and abandonment—that Christmas was not for her.

Nor was Kyle—no matter how much she fervently wished, even prayed he was.

The man had made no promises, offered no commitments. He was just passing through on the way back to his real life. They'd shared a special night. She had no right to expect anything more.

So why did it still hurt so darned much?

Kyle's knock made her jump.

She twisted around, looking to make sure the lock was secure, but didn't respond.

He tried the door; the knob didn't turn.

"Meghan?"

She rested her head on the cold glass again, wishing, hoping against hope that he'd go away. Meghan felt raw and exposed. She wanted to be left alone, yet she also wanted to be held in the security of his arms, hearing the reassuring thump of his heart beneath her ear.

As confused then as she was now, Meghan had slipped from beneath their shared blanket, banked the fire, then stolen upstairs before he awoke.

Even in silence and solitude, her answers had remained elusive, like a butterfly eternally out of reach.

"I know you're in there."

His voice was low and mesmerizing, sliding through her bruised soul like soothing balm. And somehow it made things seem worse.

"We need to talk, Meghan. We can do it through the closed door if we have to. But I'd rather look at you face-to-face."

She sighed and caved in, all the while telling herself she shouldn't. Already she was learning she couldn't resist him, didn't want to deny him.

After opening the door, she moved back, protectively

folding her arms across her chest, as if the feeble attempt could shield her feelings.

"You ran away. Why?"

To save myself.

She met his gaze, her mouth dry. He hadn't shaved yet, and the shadow only made his eyes appear darker, more intense. And pulse-thunderingly sexy.

In a few steps, Kyle vanquished the distance separating them. She stood her ground, refusing to retreat, even though an inner voice urged just that.

When he took her shoulders in his achingly tender grasp, she struggled to remain rational instead of succumbing to the emotion that charged through her.

Tilting her head back, she looked up at him. His eyes were searching, as if trying to comprehend the incomprehensible. How could she possibly explain that which she didn't understand herself?

Grasping for a logical reason for leaving his arms, she said, "I needed to work." Even Meghan heard the falseness in the words.

He swung his glance around the room and summed up his refute in a solitary, succinct word.

Her mouth dropped.

Her tender lover of the night before had disappeared. "If you'd been working, your table would have more than that angel on it."

Proving he didn't miss a single thing, he added, "And your eyes wouldn't be swimming with tears."

"They aren't." Her voice cracked.

His manner changed again just as instantly. He was the Kyle she knew—the Kyle she cared for.

Purposefully, he swept his index finger up to her lashes, transferring a drop of moisture from her onto him. "They are."

She needed to tell him something, but couldn't, wouldn't

tell him everything...couldn't allow him to access her deepest secret by learning she'd started to fall in love with him.

"We made love last night." His fingers caressed her, in the manner of a man who'd discovered what made her pulse thunder.

"Yes," she whispered.

"And when I woke up," Kyle said softly, "you weren't there. I made some breakfast, did a few chores outside, fed your mangy mutt and horse...."

She offered a tentative smile.

"And waited."

Her smile faded.

"I figured maybe you were getting dressed, or showering. I thought you might be working. But then I heard you pacing." He brushed aside another traitorous tear. "It didn't take long to realize you'd run away. And it took even less time to figure I'm part of the reason."

His captive gaze refused to turn hers loose. Blood rushed through her veins, and she knew she'd never be able to deny this man anything. She wouldn't want to.

"So how about it, Meghan?" His motions stilled. "After all we've shared, don't you think I deserve some answers?"

Ten

"**I** can't do this," Meghan confessed.

"Can't do what?"

"This…any of it. I appreciate what you're trying to do, really, but it won't work."

It would work, Kyle silently vowed. He'd make sure of it. "You agreed I could try," he said. "I'm holding you to it. Trust me."

He noticed the way her lower lip trembled. Unable to resist the draw, he placed his thumb beneath it, soothing away the betrayal of her feelings.

"Will you do that?" he asked.

"Kyle…"

"You have nothing to lose. Everything to gain."

He held a beautiful woman who teetered on the edge of tears, and he didn't have a clue what to say or how far to push. Weeping females weren't his forte. And to be honest, he'd had little experience figuring out a woman's emotional needs.

Until now he hadn't even cared to try.

He held her gaze captive, along with her body. Lord, it felt so right to hold her, cherish her. Meghan was an added reason not to continue home. He'd been reluctant to return before...now, he wanted to leave Meghan even less.

He knew that, when he left, he would take with him plenty of mental snapshots. He only hoped they would be enough to keep him company through Chicago's chillingly cold winter months, and worse, their damnably lonely nights.

Kyle decided to stockpile as many more mental keepsakes as time permitted, storing them deep inside where he could take them out and savor them later. That meant he had to take action, shatter the silence, even if he only made things worse.

"Don't cut me out, Meghan." Efficiently he sorted through his options and, in his typical way, settled for the most risky. Might as well gamble it all. "Get dressed," he said. "And wear warm clothes."

She frowned.

"We're going to find a tree to decorate."

Silence.

He mentally swore. He'd blown it. Nothing existed now, except to brazen it out.

"Kyle, look...I don't do Christmas."

Her eyes begged him to understand. He clearly comprehended only one thing: he had to touch her life, leave her as affected as he'd been.

"Didn't. You didn't do Christmas," he corrected her. "Until now, until yesterday. Get dressed," he repeated. "Or I'll drag you outside in your robe."

Her mouth formed a very kissable O. He very nearly forgot his dictate and succumbed to temptation.

"You wouldn't," she said.

"Try me." He released her shoulders, checked his watch, then folded his arms across his chest.

"You're serious."

"Yep."

Her head was tilted back, eyes sparking the same golden daggers they did when he'd aroused her in a different way.

Passion.

Its color was gold. Its name was Meghan.

Carefully, she enunciated the words, "I don't want a tree in my house."

"Fifteen minutes. I'll meet you in the kitchen." He turned on his heel and strolled from the room, wincing at the sound of her colorful words.

Downstairs, he carried armfuls of wood from the storage closet and stacked them next to the fireplace. Next he picked up the hammer, nails and screws he'd brought in earlier and rehung one of the cabinet doors. He'd be gone soon, and the more help he could give her before he left, the better.

He checked his watch. Eleven minutes had disappeared. The sound of water rushing from a distant faucet proved she was complying with his request, even if not as quickly as he hoped.

A few minutes later, she joined him. Right on time. And she didn't look too pleased about it. She wore black jeans and a white sweater that showed the swell of her breasts.

Lovely.

"I'm doing this under duress."

He kissed her. "Noted."

They dressed warmly, then he held open the back door. Snowflake bounded behind them, skidding on the ice and careering into a snowdrift. Meghan laughed, the sound natural, no pretense. It was so her. Totally appealing to his senses. How could any other woman ever compare?

Yet he knew that's exactly what he would do. Compare.

And he instinctively knew no woman would meet the incredibly high standard set by Meghan.

Kyle grabbed an ax and saw from the barn while she stroked Aspen's nose. The horse whinnied, nudging her owner. What would it be like, he wondered absently, to live here full time, away from the rat race, away from the pressures and stress that came with running a multimillion-dollar-a-year business?

Yeah. He sighed. The rat race...where the only ones who won were the rats themselves.

"Ready?" he asked.

Together they trudged through the snow. The wind had died down sometime during the night. Bright sunshine brushed across the blue sky, making the day look warmer than the temperature gauge read.

Meghan was silent, although laughter had removed the mutinous expression she'd worn earlier. They crossed the meadow, Kyle breaking a path through the foot-and-a-half-deep snow, then began up the slope, toward the trees.

"It's hard to believe Mother Nature unleashed her fury so recently," she said softly, reverently. "Yesterday, the sky was gray. Today there's only a couple of clouds, and they look as threatening as cotton balls."

He nodded.

"Isn't it incredible?"

Last night, as she'd slept in his arms, bottom snuggled against his middle, and again as he waited for her to dress, Kyle had entertained a seductive idea—that of taking her to Chicago with him. Yet, watching her, the thought slipped away, like night under the pressure of a dawning day. "You love it here."

She stopped, tipped back her head and closed her eyes. "I can't imagine living anywhere else."

Nor could he picture her anywhere else.

Kyle's heart hurt.

On top of that, he remembered the slash of pain in her voice as she'd recalled memories of her childhood. Turning away from his own ache, he said, "You've lived in a lot of places."

"Big cities, mainly, and we vacationed all over the world."

"And?"

She looked at him. "They have their own personalities, their faults, as well as their strong points. They're nice places to visit." Meghan swept her hands wide. "The native Americans call this area Land of One Hundred Skies. It's never the same, always changing. And the colors. Mauve, pink, crimson, orange. It…"

A slight stain, and not from the weather, crept to her cheeks. "Go on," he said.

"It sounds ridiculous."

He quirked his brow.

"It feeds my soul. Keeps me going…makes me wonder what the next day might hold." She was quiet for a moment, then rushed on. "There. I told you it sounded ridiculous."

"No." Kyle shook his head. "It doesn't." Maybe once, to the Kyle who lived in the depths of the concrete jungle, surrounded by the sounds of screeching tires and honking horns it might have seemed impossible, but not anymore.

He surveyed the land, trying to see it as Meghan did. In places shaded from the elements, a native grass poked up. Tracks in the snow showed that a wild animal, maybe a deer, had recently passed through. Birds sought refuge in branches, and mountaintops stretched to the sky. He'd never had the opportunity to be around someone who loved the place where they lived as much as Meghan did.

No, Chicago wasn't for her. She'd wilt there. And no matter how hard he tried, he had difficulty envisioning her as the wife of a busy executive, hostessing meaningless parties, entertaining other executives just to further his career.

He couldn't ask it of her, no matter how selfishly he might be tempted to do just that.

He sighed, a heavy sigh, from the depth of his soul. Kyle wondered how it was possible to miss something you'd never had.

In peaceful silence, they continued on until they were in the thick of the woods. The snow wasn't as deep, but a white blanket surrounded them. Limited sunlight reached the ground.

"How about that one?" Meghan asked.

He shaded his eyes and looked as she pointed to the top of a ponderosa pine. Shaking his head, he pronounced, "Too scrawny."

"That one?"

"Too big around. We'd never get it through the door."

A hawk swooped across the landscape, lighting on a tree branch and tossing snow down on top of them.

For the second time that day, the rich sound of her laughter seeped into his senses. She shook her head, sending flakes flying, and Kyle knew, in this instant, there was no place he'd rather be.

"Okay, Mr. Christmas," she said, hands teasingly propped on her hips, "since you don't like my choices—"

"Meghan, the first one was pitiful."

She laughed, and his heart stored the sight of her curved lips and twinkling eyes for the future. "Half its branches were missing," he explained.

"We could have faced the bare spot to the wall."

"The whole thing was bare."

He swung the ax from his shoulder, the head burying into the crisp powder. It was so like her to choose something that needed loving, needed a home. Much like Snowflake and that horse of hers.

"That one," she said, obviously challenging.

He surveyed the tree she wanted. Naturally, it was the tallest one with the large trunk. But he'd promised. And as he already knew, he'd do damn near anything to make her happy. "Your wish is my command." Hefting the ax, he said, "Stand back."

She moistened her lip. "Have you ever chopped down a tree?"

"Nope. How hard can it be?" When her eyebrows drew together in obvious concern, he brushed a finger down her cheekbone and relented by adding, "I'm joking. My hobby is carpentry."

"You're a carpenter?"

Why the hell had he confessed that? "Yeah." His first love. Until now, his only love.

Meghan placed her hand on his. Her expression slinked through him, feeding the place that was so hungry for her approval.

"Is carpentry a hobby, or is it something more?"

"A hobby."

"Do you wish it was something more?"

"Everyone has a dream." He shrugged. He didn't feel as philosophical about it as he pretended, but there it was.

"That's why you don't want to go home."

The icy tentacles of her words slid down his spine. She was perceptive, too perceptive by far. And her efficiently wielded words sliced through every defense he'd erected to protect himself.

"I'll survive." He knew the words were to convince himself as well as her. "It'll still be a hobby."

Kyle forcibly relegated his thoughts and her statement to the past, where they belonged, where they would stay. With a powerful stroke, he swung, sinking the ax into the flesh of the tree.

Ten minutes later, after chipping away at the trunk from

both sides, leaving a thin strip of wood to connect the top part to the bottom, he realized he'd outrun his future, for the time being. Looking at Meghan, hoping his flat refusal to discuss himself hadn't hurt her, he said, "Stand over here, just in case."

She held Snowflake by his collar. Kyle delivered a final blow, sending the pine shuddering to the ground.

Snow flew. Snowflake broke away to run in circles, barking at the fallen sentinel. A raven cawed loudly as it soared into flight.

They looked at each other for a few moments, then she said, "Impressive."

She didn't harbor resentment; for that, and a hundred other things, he appreciated her. "All in a day's work," he said. But it wasn't, he knew. It was more than that. It was what he loved, working with wood, transforming it into something special, something to bring inside to infuse the atmosphere with the sights and scents of the season.

Chopping the wood made him think of the cabin he wanted to build in northern Wisconsin, near the water, of the logs he'd already cut and notched…the cabin he would never have time to finish. And even if he did, there would be no one to share it with. Odd, before he'd met Meghan, that hadn't been a concern.

"Now what?"

"We cut a Christmas tree the perfect size, then I'll saw the rest for firewood."

After sawing for several minutes, he worked up a sweat. He took off his coat; she held it for him. Vaguely he wondered what she would do next Christmas. Buy a tree? Or maybe go without as she'd always done before.

"Kyle?"

He looked up, seeing her impish smile. Before he had time to figure out what was so funny, a snowball pelted him in the chest.

With Snowflake nipping at her heels, she darted in the direction of the house.

Dropping the saw and scooping up a handful of snow, he took off after, packing the powder as he closed the distance. The sound of her laughter spurred him on, and he let loose with the icy missile.

It splattered on her parka, but she didn't slow down. Lengthening his stride, he waited until a three-foot drift loomed in front of her, then caught her from behind in a tackle.

He twisted their bodies, managing to land beneath her. "Say uncle," he warned, holding her around the waist, imprisoning her.

Still smiling saucily, she said, "Aunt."

"I'm warning you—" Arctic cold showered from her hand onto his face. While he tried to blink the wetness from his eyes and wipe it from his mouth, she seized the opportunity to wiggle out of his embrace and flee. Snowflake gamely joined the ruckus, his excited yips adding to the noise.

Brushing away the snow with his shirtsleeve, Kyle pursued her. This time, he reached for her jacket, dragging her to a standstill. The momentum carried them both to the blanketed earth, where he effectively pinned her beneath him.

She looked up, her cheeks rosy, her smile real. Naturally, he rested in the cradle of her legs, then captured her wrists in his hand and pinned them above her head.

"Uncle," she whispered, laughing.

Snowflake nudged his leg.

"You had your chance," Kyle said just as quietly. "You didn't take it."

She blinked, then lifted her hips, trying to break his hold and escape.

He pinned her more effectively, lowering his head. "Now you have to pay the consequences."

He saw her sensual shiver.

And, back at the house, after he'd propped the tree in a metal mixing bowl filled with water, he collected from her.

Consequences.

He'd said she had to pay them. Yet he couldn't know the emotional cost to her.

Last night, Meghan had vowed to remain distant, protect her heart. Yet a single, simmering look from Kyle gave lie to the promise.

Meghan couldn't deny him, any more than she could deny herself.

And that was the worst consequence of all.

The tree stood in the corner. Soon it would be a pleasant reminder of the holiday they'd shared beneath a blizzard of snow.

Kyle closed the distance, reigniting the fire that flared outside.

Even though the house was chilled, passion stirred in her, heating her, but simultaneously exposing her emotions.

She struggled to undress as he did the same. They made it to the couch, and no farther.

He entered her swiftly, as if wanting to possess. She pushed upward with her hips, meeting him, desperate to join with him. She knew the ice she skated on was thin and cracking.

Was it so terrible to want to eradicate the pain of the past and hoard new remembrances? This couldn't last much longer. Crews would plow and sand the roads. He would roar off on the back of the Beast, returning to his responsibilities, his life.

They would each face their futures.

Alone.

Meghan lifted herself, ignoring the inner voice that warned Kyle's leaving would hurt worse than anything she'd ever experienced.

Just for now, just for this minute, she needed.

He claimed her lips. She tasted his honesty, his urgency, and most of all, the commitment she knew he was incapable of making to her.

Spent, emotionally as much as physically, Meghan dozed in his arms, feeling safe and protected. Purposefully, just for now, she pushed away intrusive thoughts of what lay ahead.

Kyle returned from the barn and hung his coat on the peg near the back door. "Okay, I found a bucket for the tree and a roll of string. Were there any ornaments in the carton?"

"One box." She held up some of the various-colored glass balls. "Twelve ornaments."

Which wouldn't go far on the eight-foot-tall tree. "That's it?"

"That and two stockings...some ribbon and wrapping paper. And a cassette of Christmas songs."

He cataloged the flash of pain that streaked across her face, touching her eyes before she managed to school it away. Before going to the barn, he'd climbed the stairs to the attic and found a carton marked Holiday Stuff. It'd been sitting next to a box bearing the words Wedding Dress. Kyle had winced, feeling as though he was trespassing in pieces of her past. Regardless, he'd carried the holiday carton to her.

Kyle had vowed to leave her with positive memories. And do it he would. Thinking, he drummed his fingers on the countertop. "Do you have popcorn? We can make it on the stove."

She frowned. "There may be a jar in the pantry, but it's pretty old. I hope it still pops."

"We're not going to eat it." His eyes narrowed as he studied her. "Don't tell me, I already know…you've never strung popcorn." When she shook her head, he said, "Do you have a needle and thread?"

"Of course."

"Then, lady, you're in for a treat."

Whistling, he found a pan and some oil, then frowned as he searched the pantry for the elusive jar.

"Top shelf," she said softly from behind him. "Or are you distracted again?"

He reached, securing her wrist in his grip. "Distracted." He stood, tugging her toward him. "Definitely distracted."

The sewing box crashed to the tile floor.

Snowflake trotted over to inspect. He sniffed, then, with a swish of his tail, he walked off, returning his attention to the tree.

The kiss was a tease, a prelude of what they'd share later. The appetizer served its purpose, whetting his desire and making her eyes fire with that tantalizing gold color.

Kyle heated the oil while she threaded the needle. It'd been so long since he'd sat in Grandma Aggie's kitchen, performing the small but significant ritual. It reminded him how much he missed her and longed for a family of his own.

And made him think how much he would like Meghan to be part of that family.

For a tantalizing moment, as kernels danced in the sizzling oil, he pictured Meghan as the mother of his children. Odd. Until now, that kind of picture had never focused in his mind.

The first kernel exploded, shattering his image along with it.

"How about cereal?"

He looked at her.

"For the tree. I have some presweetened hoops. They're all different colors." She pulled the box from the pantry. "Might help it not look so lonely."

Kyle nodded, placed the lid on the pan, then shook it, wishing that impossible tease of them sharing another Christmas together was as easy to shake.

When the popcorn was done, he carried it to the table and sat next to her, accepting the threaded needle she offered.

She stole a couple of fluffy pieces and popped them into her mouth. "Not bad," she approved.

Not bad at all, he thought, watching as she drew another from her fingers into her mouth. He reached into the pan and fed her the next few.

He felt his body ready itself for her and realized he hadn't had this kind of stamina in years. Then again, no one had ever affected him the way she did. And it went way beyond sexual, blending into the impossibility of a happily ever after.

Kyle exhaled.

He'd left Chicago searching for answers and only had more questions.

She carried the strings of popcorn and colored cereal into the living room while he wrestled with the prickly pine. Looking at her, he asked, "Where do you want it?"

Meghan gave him an impish grin.

"The tree," he clarified.

"Ah, the tree."

"Meghan, where do you want the tree?"

She pointed to the corner near the fireplace. The scent of the freshly cut pine filled the air, somehow making it seem more like Christmas. She set up the bucket he'd found and stepped back. "A few inches to the right."

Needles scratched through his flannel shirt as he moved it where she indicated.

"Too far."

He moved it back.

"Almost. A little more."

He exhaled as one of the long thin needles sank into his skin. "Meghan..."

"Perfect," she said.

Her first tree.

There was a light in her eyes he'd never seen before. He'd helped put it there, he realized, tasting the sweetness on his tongue.

"Get the string," he instructed. "Before this thing shreds me alive."

Together they worked to keep the tree straight, no easy task since the bucket wasn't designed to hold a solid, eight-foot part of the forest.

"It scratches," she protested when he asked her to keep a grip on the trunk while he drove a couple of small nails into the wall. Taking over, he had her secure the string.

When he stepped back, Meghan nodded. Then she gathered the string of popcorn. "You're taller," she said. "Can you reach the back?"

Kyle started at the top and brought the string down and around the front. She wrinkled her nose and laughed. "Make it go around."

"Thought you said you hadn't decorated a tree before."

"Good taste needs no explanation," she said. Then she moved closer to him, draping the strand. They continued on, Kyle lacing it around the back, Meghan adjusting it on the front.

Off tune, he began to sing "Deck the Halls." Gamely, but missing words and making up new ones, Meghan joined in. A surge of happiness went through him. It had been a long time since he felt this way, a very long time.

"Not bad," he approved a short time later.

They added the strands of cereal, creating a colorful combination.

"We need something for the top," she said.

"An angel."

Her eyes sparkled. "I'll be right back."

She dashed up the stairs, Snowflake barking as he followed, then returned a couple minutes later with a handful of angels. "We might as well use some of the little ones I won't be able to sell this year."

While she tied some of winged cherubs to the branches, he affixed one to the top.

"Cookies," he said.

She rolled her eyes. "You're not hungry again, are you?"

"For the tree."

"The tree's hungry?" she asked.

There it was again, the sound of her laughter. He would remember it for eternity. "The ones that didn't come out exactly right," he said, "we should hang on the tree."

"We did a good job," Meghan said twenty minutes later, folding her arms across her chest.

Stepping back, he surveyed the tree, taking in all the details. Somehow, despite the absence of glitter and glass, it was every bit as beautiful as the ones he'd had as a kid. And it meant more. Yeah. It meant more.

"We make a good team," she added.

"Yes." Kyle looked at her, taking in her smile, noticing the way her jeans snuggled her hips and thighs, and the way her body fit, so perfectly, with his. "We do."

"It's beginning to look a lot like…"

"Christmas," he said, finishing for her. Kyle reached for a small branch he'd broken off from the larger ones, then he caught her wrist and eased her closer.

"What are you doing?"

"Mistletoe."

"I may not know a lot about Christmas, Mr. Murdock, but that's definitely not mistletoe."

"It is. And I'm standing under it. And that means you have to kiss me."

"Kyle?" Gently, she rose up, tipping her head.

He inhaled the womanly scent of her perfume, it smelled of commitment and seduction.

A potent combination.

"Hmm?" he asked.

"I don't need an excuse to kiss you."

"You don't?"

She loosely tied a red ribbon around his neck, laid down the stocking in her hand, and, drawing him to her, she proved just that.

Eleven

Meghan slowly awoke.

With a yawn, she smiled and stretched. Turning on her side, she reached for Kyle. Not finding him, she opened her eyes, blinking in the bright sunshine.

Her smile froze, then faded. He wasn't there.

On Christmas Eve.

The holidays were here, and Kyle had deserted her as surely as Jack had.

Her heart turned over, and she grabbed for her robe. She listened for sounds and heard none. The house was quiet, as quiet as it had always been before Kyle's arrival.

Dread, as cold and lonely as Christmas mornings she'd known, crept over her. Meghan fought to suppress the voice that insisted he'd left without saying goodbye, telling herself that surely, after all he'd said, after the promises he'd made to her, the way he'd treated her, he wouldn't just...

Fingers trembling, she fumbled with the belt of her robe,

finally cinching it closed as she hesitantly walked into the kitchen. Pretending as though a lump hadn't formed in her throat and her pulse wasn't pounding, she pulled back the drape and looked outside.

Snowflake was pushing through the snow with his nose, tail wagging back and forth as he played. But she couldn't summon a smile. Though she'd hoped to see him, there was no sign of Kyle.

She hurried into the living room, looking for his saddle-bag, hoping beyond hope she'd find it.

A huge burst of air rushed out when she saw the black leather spread across the arm of the couch.

Until that moment, she hadn't admitted the truth, even to herself.

But now, faced with the undeniable evidence deep inside, Meghan was forced to recognize facts.

She loved Kyle.

Loved him.

Testing the feel, she pressed her hands together and whispered aloud, "I love you." Like a mist, the words floated on the coolness of early morning air. They sounded strange, but real. Honest.

Sinking onto the couch, she squeezed her eyes shut. Yes, her feelings were real and honest, but achingly worse, they were impossible.

Meghan couldn't tell him how she felt, couldn't ask him to stay. She admired his strength, his commitment to his father, his sense of obligation to the family business. Yet the traits she admired most were the things that prevented them from being together. And she cared too much about him to even suggest he give up his future, turn his back on his responsibilities all for her.

Tears welled, and forcibly, Meghan blinked them away. She wouldn't succumb. Wouldn't.

Despite her best efforts, a solitary tear slid softly down

her cheek. For a few minutes, she sat there, nursing the hurt that loving him caused.

After Jack abandoned her, Meghan had told herself she was better off alone. Funny, until now, she'd actually believed the lie.

Now she wondered how she could have fooled herself. Meghan shuddered at the idea of not hearing the gruffly male sound of Kyle's voice as he spoke her name, not inhaling the fresh, outdoorsy scent of him, not seeing the darkness in his eyes as he lowered his head for a kiss, not feeling the ripple of muscles beneath a layer of clothing.

She didn't know how much more time remained with him, but she wanted to seize every possible second. There would be wounds to nurse later—many of them. And worse, she would be faced with the irreparable damage of a heart being sliced in two.

But for now...for now, he was still here. And she wouldn't let him slip away without storing more of those memories he'd promised.

Squaring her shoulders, she resolved to do just that. Wiping her eyes, Meghan tamped down the voice warning she was opening herself to disaster.

After showering, she returned to the kitchen; this time she saw him from the window. He was crouched next to the Harley, tinkering with some wires. She turned on the kettle before putting on her warm coat. After the water boiled, she made him a cup of cocoa and carried it outside.

Snowflake bounded over, huge white paws layered with brown mud. "Don't jump," she warned.

He hung his head, and she took the time to scratch behind his ears. When she looked up, Kyle was staring at her. Her breath caught. The top button on his flannel shirt was open, providing her a tantalizing view.

"Morning," he said, voice husky and deep. The look he gave her made goose bumps chase up and down her arms.

It plainly said he recalled exactly what she'd done the night before, and that she'd spent the time with him.

The realization she wouldn't share this kind of intimacy with him after the holidays made her throat constrict.

"Morning," she said, wondering how she'd forced out the word.

"Sleep well?"

She felt a blush creep up her neck and settle on her cheeks. "No," she admitted. "I was kept awake by a very persistent male."

"Persistent, huh?"

She nodded. "Very."

"Did he, by chance, try this?" Kyle crossed to her, took the travel mug from her nerveless fingers, set it on the motorcycle seat, then placed his hands alongside her face.

Kyle claimed a kiss, making her toes curl in her boots. When he slowly drew away, she managed to gasp, "Yes... that's what he tried."

He grinned. "Guess it worked."

"It worked." Slowly, her pulse rate returned to normal and she said, "I brought you hot chocolate."

"My own angel." He reached for the cup and drank from the hole in the lid. Then he looked at her over the rim. "The Harley won't start."

Her insides constricted. "I'm sorry."

"Are you?"

Their gazes locked. "No." He didn't blink, didn't allow her the escape of looking away. "No," she repeated, "I'm not sorry."

"Neither am I."

Then, with a wicked grin, he whispered a seductive suggestion on what they could do to pass the time.

A slow melt oozed down her insides, settling low and deep. Breathlessly she agreed.

* * *

"Lexie!"

Michael's voice arrived with such a force, her halo lifted and started to blow away. Lexie reached up and struggled to hold her halo on.

Grandma Aggie provided no help at all, standing there with her hands firmly clasped in front of her, appearing completely innocent, or if not, at least suitably penitent.

Aggie wouldn't confess the problem with the Harley had been her idea. Even if she did, it would appear she was covering for Lexie.

Either way, Lexie was in trouble.

Without being told, she knew she'd been assigned to guard that mangy beast, Curiosity, at least for a while longer.

Lord, she prayed, *let Meghan rediscover the joy of Christmas before it's too late. And get me away from that horrible four-footed beast.*

"Lexie, Lexie," Michael said quietly, the edges of patience seeming to fray, "you shouldn't be appealing to the higher power."

She sighed. She recognized the summons, even though it was gently phrased as a warning. Michael required an audience.

Glancing over her shoulder, she paused long enough to whisper to Grandma Aggie, "Whatever you do, stand in Kyle's way of leaving. I'll keep Michael distracted and take whatever chastisement he deems appropriate."

"Oh, Lexie!" Grandma Aggie twisted her hands, then reached for a skein of yarn and frantically began knitting.

Lexie didn't mind. Aggie appeared totally innocent, and perhaps, understandably, a bit misguided by the questionable influence of Lexie. Which meant Aggie could continue to cause trouble without Michael being aware of it.

"Don't let me down," she begged.

Grandma Aggie nodded.

Straightening her halo, Lexie then blew a bubble and snapped her gum, feigning a confidence she was nowhere close to feeling.

"I'll hold on to you," Kyle swore. "Promise."

She worried her lower lip, the same lip he'd tasted earlier. He still recalled its texture and surrender.

"Are you sure?" she asked.

"Would I do anything to hurt you?"

Meghan looked up at him. Kyle saw a veil of question in her hazel eyes, but it vanished quickly, making him wonder if it had been a trick of the sunshine, or if she was hiding something.

He blinked, pushing away his ludicrous thought.

"That's a long way down," she said, pointing toward the steep hill they'd traversed.

He held up the ancient sled he'd found in the barn and repaired earlier. "Are you questioning my carpentry skills, or my protective skills?"

"You're a great carpenter."

"Ah, so you're not sure I can take care of you."

"That's not it."

She shook her head, the layers of her blond hair teasing her face and neck. Giving in, he feathered them back, letting his thumb pause on the pulse that pounded in her throat.

Even as he felt the number increase, his pulse did likewise. He'd never been as affected by a woman as he was by Meghan. She'd gotten to him. She made him laugh, think, care.

He'd started out wanting to give her Christmas. And he'd ended up as the beneficiary of the experience. In showing her what she was missing, he'd rediscovered those very same things himself.

"I'll sled with you," she said softly. "I trust you."

His heartbeats thundered, slamming into overdrive. *Trust.* What an incredible word, filled with meaning and hope.

He'd never heard it before...savored it now.

"Have a seat."

She looked at the small sled, the steep slope, then back at him. "Are you sure about this?"

"Thought you said you trusted me."

"I do." She clenched her teeth. "But..."

"Are you chicken?" he challenged.

"Chicken? Me?"

He nodded. "Are you?"

She maneuvered herself onto the sled. He chuckled and choked back the sound when he saw her reach for a handful of snow. "Didn't think you were," he said. "Chicken, that is. Not you. Definitely not you."

He climbed on the sled, sitting behind her, then adjusting them both so that her behind rested snugly between his thighs. She lifted one of her buttocks, then sashayed backward, bringing him to instant arousal. "Meghan," he warned.

Then she did it again.

He was adjusting himself to be more comfortable when she blasted him with the snow she'd scooped up.

"Teach you to call me a chicken."

"I took it back."

"Not soon enough." She laughed.

He leaned to the side to reach for his own missile. The movement tipped them off balance, sending the sled careering. She screamed, a sound of exhilaration rather than fear. Adrenaline thundered and he adjusted his legs, trying to control the out-of-control runners.

They tipped over, rolling together down the hill.

Her eyes were open wide, her lips formed a line somewhere between amusement and shock, and her arms were laced tightly around his neck.

He protected her the best he could, and Snowflake chased after them, barking frantically.

Near the bottom, they came to a stop. Kyle landed on top. He rested between her spread thighs, saw the rapid rise and fall of her chest.

Reaching up, she stroked a glove-covered index finger down the side of his cheek. "I like the way you sled," she said cheekily, rocking her hips upward. "Let's do it some more."

After trekking to the top, they did.

This time, they positioned themselves carefully, making sure they had equal weight distribution.

"Ready?" he asked.

She nodded.

He pushed them off and her laughter rang in his ears. As they gained speed, her hair flew out behind her, and she snuggled back, seeking the protection he so gladly offered.

After a few more runs, he stood, then offered his hand, helping her up. As he pulled her up, she winced.

"Stiff?" he asked.

"Splinter," she corrected him. She twisted, glancing over her shoulder.

"Isn't this your second in just a couple of days?"

"Thanks for the reminder...you're such a gentleman."

He followed the direction of her gaze. "In your thigh?"

Meghan shook her head. "My rear. And I can't see it through my jeans."

"You have a splinter in your butt?"

She looked at him and frowned. "That wasn't exactly how I put it," she protested.

"I look forward to getting it out."

"You would."

"Yeah," he agreed, fanning his hand across the small of her back. "I would."

And back at the house, he did. "This isn't a splinter," he remarked as she lay on the couch, stomach pressed into the soft cushions. "It's more like a branch. Maybe we could hang some ornaments from it."

"Beast!"

He smoothed his palm over her soft, pale flesh. She pushed off the couch slightly, as if seeking more of his touch. "This is firing my imagination, Meghan," he said.

"Kyle?"

"Hmm?"

"Get the splinter out."

"Splinter?"

"What did you think you're doing back there?"

"Honey, I'd be happy to show you." He trailed his fingers between her naked thighs, stroking her intimately, even as she arched toward him.

"Uh, Kyle…can we get the splinter out first?"

She shifted in her seat, muscles cramped from sitting so long…well, that along with the enthusiastic lovemaking she and Kyle shared. She felt a hot flush staining her face at the memory of how they'd last joined, and she sought to suppress a secret smile.

Meghan thanked her lucky stars that she'd never thrown away that last box of condoms she and Jack never had occasion to use. After all, Kyle's meager supply hadn't lasted as long as he had.

Rubbing the small of her back and trying to bring her thoughts back to the present, Meghan blew out a puff of air, then leaned back in her seat to survey her handiwork.

The angel Meghan had been working on as a surprise Christmas present—as well as goodbye gift—for Kyle was beautiful. Grandma Aggie, as Meghan had named the four-inch cherub, was special.

Meghan was her own worst critic, but even she recognized that the sculptured angel, hands folded together and wearing a serene smile, was beautiful. In fact, Grandma Aggie was the best one Meghan had ever made. Alive with love and animation, Grandma Aggie was an appropriate thank-you to the man who'd given her so much.

Kyle had said previously that his grandmother had green eyes, and that's exactly what Meghan gave the clay namesake. The angel's eyes were cast downward, and Meghan picked up the piece, signing her name to the bottom and adding a title, Watching Over You.

She reached for her hot glue gun and placed a satin ribbon, red to serve as a reminder of the Christmas season they shared. A few wayward tears blurred her vision. She hoped, in the coming years, Kyle would think of her when he saw the angel. It would provide a connection that time and distance could never sever.

And she knew, with just as much conviction, time and distance wouldn't destroy the love she felt for him.

"Meghan?"

She heard his distinctive footfall on the stairs and grabbed a towel to cover the angel. Rushing, she met him in the hallway, pulling the door closed behind her. He frowned but said nothing.

"I warmed up some more pasta," he said. "Thought you might be hungry."

"I am. Thanks."

All through their simple meal, hardly a word was exchanged. The simmering look he shot her made her insides twist, killing her appetite.

Her nerves were on edge, emotions taut. Tomorrow was Christmas morning, the one day of the year that always brought hurt and disillusionment. And Kyle would leave soon.

She'd already heard the distant and just as unmistakable sounds of huge plows clearing the two-lane highway. Yet, no matter how she wanted to protect herself, she was completely vulnerable to him. A single look made her want, a touch flooded her with desire.

How was it possible, she wondered, to willingly expose yourself to another human being, even knowing the only possible outcome was pain?

While he washed dishes, she took a bath, hoping the hot water might warm her insides, as well as her body.

She joined him downstairs, escaped tendrils of hair teasing her neck, curling on her forehead. She'd wrapped a robe around her naked body, not bothering with a nightgown or panties. He'd have them off her soon enough, anyway.

"Come here."

He offered his hand from where he knelt near the fire. The scent of wood smoke blended with his freshness. Stubble shaded his chin and made his eyes appear darker. Pine crackled and sparked, emitting an intimate glow.

She moved toward him, placed her hand in his, then knelt. He trailed kisses down her throat, then bared her shoulder an agonizing fraction of an inch at a time.

He shimmered the fabric from her, and she saw the way his eyes sparked in the firelight. Passion. When she was before him, wearing nothing at all, he grabbed a few pillows and plumped them. He lowered her to the pillows, and she reached for him, taking his sex in her hand and moving back and forth gently. He was hard, responsive. As he bit out a groan, she increased the pressure and speed.

"Meghan…"

She ignored the warning.

Kyle cursed, settling his hand over hers and stopping her movements. Still, she held him, reveling in the feel of his pure masculinity. Kyle reached for a wrapped condom and dropped it in his haste. She inhaled sharply, filled with awe that she'd made him as hungry for her as she was for him. "Here," she said, picking up the package.

Releasing him for a second, she removed the protection. "Can I?" she asked hesitantly.

"Sure." The word was long and drawn out as she placed the condom on him and slowly began to unroll it.

Finally, sheathed, he entered her. She met him, motion for motion, crying out a little at the depth of his penetration. She wanted, wanted more.

He reached his own satisfaction, then, a minute or so later, his weight propped on his elbows, looked down at her. "Your turn."

"But...I mean, I...earlier I..."

His expression was set in lines of determination. Capturing her hands in one of his, he raised them above her head. Her nipples naturally thrust upward, and as the warmth of his breath fanned across her breasts, she strained toward him, desperate to seize his promise...and to hold it forever. After all, she knew exactly what the morning held.

And that scared her more than anything else ever had.

Afterward, when he was certain of her satiation, he held her close.

She must have slept, because a sound, shattering the silence, woke her with a start.

"The heater," he said, wrapping his arm more fully around her.

She blinked. "The power's back on?"

He nodded.

The return of electricity meant half a dozen different things. They wouldn't have to share the same blankets near the fireplace just to stay warm.

She gulped for a breath. Soon there'd be no reason for Kyle to remain with her.

It was small of her, and she'd known she shouldn't have placed her fragile belief in his word, but she didn't want to lose him...especially not when dawn would bring Christmas Day.

Warmth spilled from the overhead heating vents and Snowflake crashed the cans from the kitchen cupboards. Meghan tried not to think at all, acting as though her heart wasn't hurting, and grabbed for her robe.

She had to be alone. Escape.

Kyle followed her into the kitchen, wearing unzipped jeans and a frown. "Are you okay?"

She looked at him, tried for a breezy air. "Fine. Just thought I'd feed the dog."

"Meghan."

She'd failed. Breezy wasn't her style, disguising her emotions was next to impossible.

"You ran away. Again. You accused me of doing the same thing, but you run every time you don't want to face me."

"I was just—"

"Meghan," he interrupted, voice matching the rigid stance. "No excuses, just the truth."

He flipped a switch, flooding the kitchen with nearly two-hundred watts of light. Kyle wouldn't allow her to run, even hide.

She moistened her lower lip. He might be wearing very few clothes, but his body language was anything but casual. The steel blue reflected in the depths of his eyes gave her a glimpse of the powerhouse he was, the formidable opponent he could be.

"Correct me if I'm wrong..." He trailed off. His gaze pinioned hers, and his intensity held her captive. She tried to look away and failed. "But didn't we just make love?"

She gulped. "Yes."

Her mind raced as she frantically sorted through her options. How much to tell him? He would see through lies and wouldn't tolerate them. Still, she had to protect herself, along with her heart, no matter how difficult that might be when Kyle consumed the atmosphere around them.

"And didn't you enjoy it?"

Scarlet heated her face.

"Then you owe me an explanation."

She nodded, stalling.

"We can sort through anything, together." He folded his arms across his chest, emphasizing the breadth of him, the power of him.

Anything except this, she realized. Because nothing could change the future. And nothing could mend a broken heart.

"Meghan? I'm waiting."

Twelve

Kyle drummed his fingers on the counter and watched honest emotions play across Meghan's face.

He'd been right earlier, he had glimpsed something—pain, perhaps—that she wanted to keep hidden from him. Her face was expressive, and he cared enough to pry. This time he was determined they wouldn't leave the kitchen until he received the answers he wanted.

Meghan looked at him, eyes wide, bottom lip swollen from where she'd worried it. The layers of blond hair framed her face, making her seem even more innocent, more vulnerable.

She twisted her hands in her robe, threading the fabric between her fingers. But when she spoke, Kyle knew it would be with the same honesty that was reflected in her eyes.

He waited.

Tree branches swayed in the wind, reaching out to the windowpane, heightening the already-thick tension.

She blinked several times; he watched the internal battle that raged inside her. Her brows had furrowed and her shoulders hunched forward, a scant inch or two. Obviously she wanted to protect herself and, just as obviously, knew he wouldn't settle for anything less than the whole truth.

Since he'd arrived, they'd been completely open and honest with each other. And it was a bond of trust—so tight and forged from the worst of circumstances—that neither dared shatter.

"You're leaving me."

His gut constricted. Breath rushed out in a painful exhalation, as if she'd sunk her elbow into his stomach.

She hadn't done that, exactly, he realized.

And the result was worse. She'd hurt him, caught him where he was the weakest...his heart.

Her words were well chosen, succinct and sword sharp. They pierced him with laser-sighted accuracy, sucking out rational thought along with reason.

He squeezed his eyes shut and felt a frown settle on his forehead.

Christmas should have been filled with anticipation and joy. In fact, those were the gifts he'd desperately wanted to give her.

Instead, her expression was filled with angst, the one thing he'd vowed she wouldn't experience.

Kyle had tried to teach her the meaning of Christmas, and failed. Only a few days remained before the New Year. Kyle had promised he'd be in Chicago to succeed his father. The minute the Harley fired, he'd be on his way. Even at the expense of his cutting out his own heart.

Opening his eyes, he saw teeth slicing into her bottom lip. Still, that didn't stop the trembling. He swore silently, a vicious word that still wasn't strong enough.

Tearing out his heart didn't hurt half as bad as the expression of betrayal in her compelling eyes.

He wanted to erase it, vanquish it forever, along with the other pain she'd suffered. Yet the thing she needed most was the one he was incapable of giving: a future.

Kyle knew, with sudden clarity, the cross-country trip had been a bad choice. Now, more than ever, he didn't want to return home...didn't want to lose Meghan.

"Come to Chicago with me."

Her eyes widened, betrayal replaced by shock.

The rash offer surprised him as much as her. Now that it was spoken, he realized that, no matter how wrong it sounded, no matter how he'd sworn to himself he wouldn't ask it of her, it needed to be said.

He wanted her with him—needed her with him—for all time. To love and cherish, and all those sentiments that at one time seemed so meaningless.

"Go to Chicago?"

Kyle nodded. His gut churned with anticipation as well as fear.

A wayward tear spilled from the corner of her eye. Slowly, she shook her head. "I can't." A sob caught in her throat, corresponding with the one that suddenly lodged near his Adam's apple.

"My life is here," she whispered, the scratch of anguish slicing through his defenses. She placed a hand against her chest, as if warding off the allure of impossibility. "I can't live in the big city. I can't do it all over again. I survived once...." She blinked. "Please don't ask me to try again."

He'd known he didn't have the right to ask that of her.

"Don't worry about me," she said, the words cloaked in a sheen of bravery. She moved toward him, traced her fingertips down the side of his face, pausing in the cleft of his chin. "You made no promises."

"Meghan, don't—"

"It's okay," she interrupted. She swallowed, then said,

"We were both lonely...an affair was natural under the circumstances, it's not like—"

"Don't." Anger, hot, biting, more powerful than anything he'd ever felt, spiked through him.

He clamped her wrist with his hand, then grabbed one of her shoulders, holding her prisoner. His next words were clipped. "Don't you dare cheapen what we had, what we have, by calling it an affair."

She met his stare, not blinking. He admired her courage, as much as he despised her words.

"What *do* you call it?" she softly challenged.

She stood her ground, tilting her head back to look at him squarely. He noticed her swallow deeply, the only betrayal of how much he affected her.

"Damn it, Meghan, it's more than an affair."

"Is it?"

He became aware of the fact he held her tightly, and even though she hadn't protested, he was probably hurting her. Kyle forced himself to relax his hold, although a less sane part of him wanted her to hurt as much as he did.

That was another new feeling for him. Women never got to him that way. He'd never been concerned about a woman enough to want to inflict pain.

Until now.

Until Meghan.

He cared. Yeah, not much doubt about it. But he didn't dare name his feelings as anything more, as anything deeper. Soon he'd be on his way, this time would become the ghost of a Christmas past.

Frighteningly he had a thought of Christmas future—without Meghan, without anyone special to share the holiday. Another endless round of parties. Oh, Pam and Mark would invite him over, he had no doubt. He'd bounce Raymond and Whitney on his knees, all the while knowing they couldn't fill the hole in his heart where his own kids should be.

The sound of Meghan's voice penetrated, and he blinked.

"Let's just take the good experiences and remember them," she said, being stronger than he could. "It's been a special time. I thank you for it."

He settled his mouth over hers, demanding from her body a commitment neither were free to make.

Swinging her into his arms, Kyle carried her to the living room, flipping off the lights as he went.

Their lovemaking went far beyond a physical act, it transcended into the emotional, alternately tender and desperate, and always passionate.

When he found his release, he felt only one thing. Regret. Regret for what might have been, regret for what never would be. Regret that they would go their separate ways.

He held her tight and felt a drop of moisture on his chest.

With sadness he eased it onto his fingertip and identified the wetness as Meghan's tears.

"You'll stay for dinner?"

Kyle nodded tightly. "If you made enough for two."

She released the breath that she had bottled up inside.

Earlier, before he started working on his motorcycle, he'd brought in the refrigerator items from the barn, including a small turkey. Meghan had purchased it for Thanksgiving and never cooked it. As she'd looked at the bird on that Thursday morning, she'd realized there was no point in preparing a feast for one—she was alone, just like on every other holiday.

She was glad she had the turkey for today's meal, her first real Christmas dinner.

No, that wasn't exactly true. Today's dinner wouldn't be a real Christmas dinner…not with the pall of loneliness that loomed at the end of the day.

In fact, this promised to be the worst one of all.

"Did..." She trailed off, cleared her throat of the ache that seemed perpetually lodged there and began again, "Did your motorcycle start?"

"Yeah. On the first try."

She was unprepared for the way her heart twisted. They'd made love with enormous passion last night, and she'd known instinctively that the recollection of it had to last a lifetime.

Since Kyle's arrival, she'd discovered love. She'd thought at first it was a rediscovery, but learned that wasn't the truth at all. She'd never loved Jack, certainly not with this kind of intensity.

Last night, Kyle had offered the opportunity to tell him what resided inside. She'd been unable to do it. But for a fragment of a moment she'd been tempted...oh, so tempted, and nearly accepted the wild proposal of traveling to Chicago with him.

Common sense had reared its unwelcome head, warning her of all the possible pitfalls.

Yet, when the light went out of his eyes, she'd barely bitten back the words that would have sent her with him. What scared her the most was if he'd said he loved her, nothing—nothing—could have stopped her from going with him. For Kyle, she would sacrifice anything.

"I'm going to clean up before we eat."

He stopped, instead of brushing by her. Leaning forward, he gave her a quick kiss on the forehead. His former intensity was gone, and awkwardness resided in its place. They were no longer lovers. Never again would they share their innermost secrets or fears.

As she set the table, she heard water rushing through pipes. Kyle's presence pervaded the atmosphere; everywhere she looked there were mental reminders of him. She'd entered the bathroom this morning, finding his toiletries mixed with hers. It spoke of intimacy…intimacy that would fracture in mere minutes.

Wildly she wished he'd quietly left before she woke up. That would have been cruel, but torturing herself like this was far, far worse.

She drained the potatoes and mashed them, noting the absence of sound. Kyle had obviously finished his shower. Snowflake slinked into the kitchen, nails clicking on the tile. He lay down at Meghan's feet, dropping his head onto outstretched paws with a little whine, as if sensing her melancholy.

When Kyle entered to the kitchen, she turned, summoning a false smile. In the past, she'd had plenty of practice hiding her feelings. Today wouldn't be any different.

For shameless seconds, she inhaled the shower-fresh crispness of him, saw the way red-and-green-plaid flannel—she wondered if the color was chosen in honor of the day—hugged his shoulders and stretched across his chest, and noted the way dark denim conformed to his thighs. He'd shaved. The lack of an evening shadow emphasized the square set of his jaw, along with the appealing cleft in his chin.

She knew today would definitely be different. Hiding her feelings would require huge amounts of emotional energy…she hoped she still had some left.

"Smells good. Anything I can do to help?"

"Carve the turkey?"

With a few controlled motions, he made even slices, then served them. Trying to act nonchalantly, she carried potatoes, cranberry sauce and corn to the table, then sat across from him.

He said a brief blessing, and she added her own silent, impossible hopes for a Christmas miracle.

"This is wonderful," he said approvingly. "Thanks."

Because she had to, she took a few obligatory bites.

When none of the food had a distinguishable taste, she placed her fork alongside her plate.

Twenty minutes later, as Kyle folded his napkin, she again reminded herself she'd mastered the art of disguising her private thoughts.

She'd had no ingredients for pie; even if she did, her pie crusts never turned out right. Still, she was reluctant to let him go and wanted to prolong their parting as long as possible. "Can I make you some hot chocolate?"

Their gazes met, locked. He shook his head. Even though she'd suspected he would refuse, she wasn't prepared for the stinging blow his words delivered. "I'm burning daylight. I'd like to make it to Denver by dusk."

"I see."

"Meghan, I'm sorry, I never meant—"

"Don't," she interrupted, her voice low. Her stomach was twisted into tiny, painful knots.

"I checked the phones this morning. Service has been restored." He continued to regard her. "I called Pam, my sister."

She nodded, encouraging him to continue, even as each word made her die a little more.

"They're holding off their celebration until I arrive home."

She summoned a smile that lasted less time than a shooting star. Using his words, since she couldn't find any of her own, she said, "You're burning daylight."

"Yeah."

Meghan moistened her lower lip, then wondered how that was even possible with her mouth being so dry. "Before you go, I have something I'd like to give you," she said.

He arched his brows.

"A...a Christmas present. I'll be right back."

She took the stairs slowly, trying to drag out each remaining second. Meghan picked up the box, then taped on a satin bow she'd tied herself.

When she met him downstairs, his jacket hung across the couch, gloves and saddlebag sitting across the leather.

"You didn't need to do this," Kyle said.

"I wanted to."

He accepted the box. Their fingertips brushed, and the jolt of awareness seemed to make her already experience the shock of his absence.

He carefully slid a finger under the bow and removed it. Then he used his blunted thumbnail to slice through the piece of tape sealing the package.

Time hung suspended as she waited for his reaction.

He pulled out the tissue-wrapped figurine, unwrapping it slowly. For long moments, he didn't look up. Instead, he traced the outline of the halo, seemingly lost in thought.

Meghan twisted her hands together. None of the other angels she'd ever made meant as much as Grandma Aggie. "Well?" she finally asked, voice breathless from anticipation.

"Meghan, it's..." He met her gaze, then coughed. She wondered if it was to cover the emotion that was reflected in the depths of his eyes.

"It's remarkable." He cleared his throat.

This time, she did see a sheen that might have been named tears.

"It looks just like my grandmother. You captured her expression." Breaking contact with her gaze, he touched his finger to the figurine's nose. In his hands, the angel looked so tiny, so fragile. "I'll cherish it," he said.

She believed he would. "It has a name," she said. "On the bottom."

He turned it, read the name she'd inked in.

"Lady, you're incredible."

Kyle placed a gentle kiss on her forehead, saying with actions what he couldn't with words.

Then he rewrapped the gift, taking a shirt from his saddlebag and rolling the clay angel in it for protection.

His hand seemed to pause over the saddlebag, then she heard him clear his throat. After a few long seconds, he turned back to her.

"I have something for you," Kyle said. As he looked at her, she wondered if it was a trick of the light that made it again appear as if emotion glistened in his eyes. It had to be a trick, Meghan realized, Kyle didn't care about her nearly as much as she cared for him.

He dug under his jacket, pulling out a gift, wrapped in the comics section of a newspaper. Offering her the present he shrugged, and said, "I didn't have any real wrapping paper."

A fragile smile formed, and she prayed she could maintain the facade just a few minutes longer. With as much care as he'd shown, Meghan removed the paper. Hands trembling at the sight of the intricately carved wooden angel, she sucked in a breath.

He'd etched in the subtle details that animated the carving. The wings appeared to be made of three-dimensional feathers, layered one on top of the other. He'd given her eyes, cheeks, a mouth, and a robe that appeared to be flowing. Her hands were folded in prayer, her head tilted downward humbly. "You made this?"

"Merry Christmas, Meghan."

"It's stunning." She forced herself to breathe, then added, "Simply gorgeous." He'd said carpentry was a hobby; he hadn't said it was a gift.

"She's hollow, so she can sit on top of the tree."

"An angel—"

"To watch over *you*," he added.

She crossed to him, giving him a deep kiss, her thanks

for the present, as well as for the time they'd shared. "Before you go, will you help me put her in place?"

"Sure."

Meghan rose onto tiptoes. Kyle removed the angel already in place, then eased the top part of the tree toward her. Pine needles scratched her as she slid his gift onto her perch. Stepping back, she surveyed the angel. She did appear to be watching over them.

"I love her, Kyle." Meghan ached to say the words directly to him, but didn't possess the bravery to allow her to face a stinging rejection. No—it was better she let him go, without displaying the emotion that might embarrass her, and maybe him in the process.

"I was serious about giving you a start in business."

She nodded, doubting he'd even remember her after he passed the Leaving Colorful Colorado sign.

"Do you have a business card?"

"No, but I'll write my number on a piece of paper."

"Wait." He extracted his wallet and removed a couple of his cards. "Write your number on this."

After she did, he reached for her pen, then scribbled a number on the back of another card. "This is my private line."

She accepted the small piece of paper stock. Kyle's fingers clamped on her shoulders as he added, "I want you to call if you need anything—anything. Understand?"

"Promise," she lied.

"You'll ship the fifty angels I'm buying?"

She nodded.

"I'll be in touch about Pam's store. By this time next year we'll have you up and going with nationwide distribution. You'll have a comfortable income, and more orders than you can fill."

She didn't want that, she only wanted him.

The edges of Meghan's control started to crumble. If he didn't leave, she would beg him to stay.

Suddenly anxious for him to be on his way, to end her agony, she reached for his coat and offered it to him.

Wordlessly he accepted, shrugging into the well-worn, butter-soft leather. It settled onto his shoulders with the comfort of a lover. Trying to distract herself, she handed him the motorcycle gloves.

Kyle stuffed in his fingers, then winced as he removed a pine needle. Crossing the room, he tossed the sharp sliver behind the fireplace grate. A fire no longer gave life to the hearth. It seemed appropriate that it should stand cold and empty.

"Kiss me goodbye?"

She should resist. Instinct urged her to run. Yet desperation, at war with her other internal urgings, for just one more moment with him, encouraged her to stay.

Meghan stood still.

His kiss tasted of the salt of her own tears, his tenderness, and shared poignancy. Meghan knew, after today, she would never again be the same.

With obvious reluctance, he ended the kiss. One hand snuck to her lips and she pushed it against them, as if she could seal in the taste of him, the warmth of him, the memory of him.

Kyle opened the door. Sunshine danced across the snow that remained on dormant earth and clung to the bare branches of trees.

It looked beautiful, and forlorn.

Without another word, he kissed her hard before striding off. He situated his pack, then swung his leg over the seat, settling the enormous machine between his thighs.

The sound of the motorcycle starting shattered the silence, sending birds scattering for sanctuary.

Their gazes collided, and she read an unspoken message in his eyes. "I'll call you," he mouthed.

She believed neither message.

Their affair had been brief, but intense, and maybe, after a long time, she could reach out and study the pieces he'd left behind. But not now...not for a very long time.

He pulled on a black helmet. Meghan knew she'd always remember him this way, dressed in black, snuggled beneath leather and wearing the aura of danger.

Raising a hand in a salute, Kyle roared off, taking her love with him.

How long she stood there, listening to the purr of a fading engine, she didn't know. She only knew it felt colder than before.

And much more lonely.

On feet that felt made of wood, she went back inside, pulling the door shut behind her.

For a second time, her stomach sank.

Snowflake's paw proudly rested on the downed Christmas tree. Cookies, cereal and popcorn were scattered everywhere, crushed between branches.

Her and Kyle's Christmas tree had toppled, and now the memories it represented lay in smashed devastation.

Snowflake whimpered, cookie crumbs clinging to his fur.

And then, when she saw it, her heart stopped.

The angel.

Meghan gave a quiet cry and hurried across the room. She sank to her knees, scooping up the angel. Gently she traced the carved wood, trying to make sure the sculpture wasn't damaged.

Thankfully there were no scratches. If only her heart felt the same way...

Holding the angel, Meghan pulled out the business card Kyle had given her. She stared at the small, impersonal reminder of him. Unable to help herself, Meghan pulled the angel closer and succumbed to the tears that had been threatening for so very long.

Tired, spent, hurt, she placed the angel near the toppled tree.

Snowflake slithered over, stopping beside her. He cocked his head to one side, an ear flopping over as he seemingly apologized for his part in her anguish. Blinking, reminding herself he'd meant no harm, she scratched the top of his head.

For long seconds, she stared at the card, the words a reminder of the man she'd loved and lost. If she couldn't have him, she didn't want the card as a constant reminder, taunting her with what might have been.

Kyle had vowed to take away the hurt and replace it with happiness. He'd given her the second, and shown her that pain was only relative to the amount of love you had for a person.

Despite her own best intentions, their Christmas together had broken her heart.

She choked on a sob.

Her internal ache was worse than any she could have ever imagined. She reached for a lighter and flicked the igniter. Snowflake whimpered when she touched the flame to the corner of the card.

Slowly, the printed words were eaten away. With fresh tears tracing her cheeks, she tossed his address and phone number into the fireplace—as barren and cold as her insides.

After all, it was Christmas Day and she was alone once more.

Thirteen

Grandma Aggie shook her head, her knitting lying in a discarded heap on top of a cloud. "But…"

Lexie looked at the crestfallen expression on Aggie's face, then wrapped the other angel in the protective folds of her wings. Lexie didn't know what to say. She'd been so sure everything would work out, so convinced. It was a match made in heaven—or at least it was supposed to have been.

A tear formed in Lexie's eyes, corresponding to the anguish inside her charge. No doubt about it, Lexie had failed, miserably. She deserved whatever consequences were meted out. In trying to make Meghan happy, Lexie had only succeeded in hurting both Meghan and Kyle.

As Lexie's tear hardened into a diamond, she vowed never again to interfere in earthly matters.

Kyle stopped in the sleepy town of Jefferson, intent on topping off the gas tank before attempting Kenosha Pass. Naturally, the town's only service station was closed.

A tired-looking wreath adorned the ancient door, that and the Closed sign were the only visible reminders that today was Christmas Day.

Lifting the kickstand, Kyle headed east, toward Denver, eventually toward Chicago.

He eased the bike toward the pass, and as he rounded a curve in the road, banked by a huge drift of snow, he caught a glimpse of the valley below.

From this vantage, he saw the huge vista, the meadow blanketed in white. Pure blue skies dipped behind distant mountain peaks, and sunlight danced across the snow that sparkled on pine branches, weighing them down. A few high clouds swirled a message of holiday hope and peace.

At the next bend, Kyle pulled onto the shoulder, stopped and removed his helmet. Cold air rushed to meet him, but the sun's rays filtered through the atmosphere and warmed the exposed skin.

Thoughts of Meghan crowded his mind. He tried to stop them, tried to push them away, finally, tried to ignore them, but there they were.

He recalled how she looked the first time he saw her, cream-colored leggings, a pastel pink sweater and a frown of distrust. Through their time together, that expression had faded completely, replaced by others: caring, passion and...

He grasped for it.

Love.

Could it have been love?

He had learned to read passion in the way her eyes darkened with spikes of gold, read the happiness in impishly upturned lips, read her hesitation by the way she incessantly worried that lower lip.

But love?

It wasn't possible. Was it?

She needed a keeper. He'd thought that when she opened the door and turned to chase after Snowflake. Through the days, as he'd made repairs to the barn and house, he'd had the same thought another dozen times.

And as for business… She had talent, vast amounts of it, but didn't have the inclination or time to pursue the money-making end of her business.

If she had someone to share the load, she could be so much more than she already was. She needed a keeper. She needed…

Him.

Kyle instantly rejected the idea.

It couldn't be him.

Yet the possibility of another man stepping into the role he'd so briefly filled made him flinch with pain. Selfishly, he didn't want anyone else to have her. But damn it, she needed someone. She needed…

Him.

This time, he didn't reject the idea; instead, he allowed it to tease and tantalize, playing in a future that had, until this moment, seemed impossible.

He thought of the way Meghan's eyes had misted when he left. Her expression, so honest and real, had revealed her inner thoughts. His leaving, especially on Christmas Day, had shattered her heart.

And that was the absolute last thing he ever wanted to do.

Kyle cursed, the word drifting as a puff on the cold, thin mountain air. He'd tried to teach her the true meaning of Christmas, but had only shown her the external trappings; out-of-tune songs, strung popcorn and fresh-cut trees, along with improvised mistletoe.

But none of them were the real meaning. Love.

And in the process, he'd taught her only one thing, that her fears and disillusionment were real.

He had no right to do that to her.

No right to do that to them.

He sat his helmet on the back of the seat as breath burned from his lungs. In the last few days, teacher had become student, for she'd taught him how to love.

Until this second, he hadn't recognized that fact. Jeez. He loved her.

He *loved* Meghan...wanted her to be his wife, wanted her to share her future, wanted to create life with her.

Leaving her hurt—bad. And it wasn't because of what he faced, it was because of what he'd lost.

Kyle plowed spread fingers through his hair.

He'd left Chicago on a search, had spent weeks on the road, then found the answers he sought in a quiet farmhouse tucked away from the world. By all rights, he shouldn't have found her in the huge world. It was as if something, something special had brought them together.

And he knew with a certainty, they were meant to be together.

Damn the consequences.

Kyle had always done what was expected of him, attended the schools he was supposed to, played the right sports, took the right number of credit hours, pulled in the expected grades, taken a job with his father's company after graduation, and dated the "right" women. And never had he done anything for himself.

This time was different. Murdock Enterprises was his father's one and only love, it sure as hell wasn't Kyle's. Miles could do what he wanted with the business, even sell it to the highest bidder. It didn't matter to him. Only one thing mattered: Meghan.

A hawk screeched across the sky, seeming to echo his sentiment.

Love. Kyle had tasted the thrill of its power, its pull, its allure, its promise. Love. Its name was Meghan.

Kyle grabbed his helmet, determined to reach her quickly, intent to beg her to be his wife...if she would have him.

He drove fast, nudging past the speed limit. It was Christmas, and he had a final gift to offer her.

When no one answered his knock, he tried the knob. It turned and the door opened. A keeper. She definitely needed a keeper. He grinned—this time determined that man would be him.

He noticed the tree first, crashed to the floor. His grin faded and his gut twisted as he thought of the hurt she must have felt when she saw it.

Walking in farther, he saw her. Without moving, he watched her for a few seconds. Snowflake lay near her, on the floor. The protective mutt merely looked up and wagged his tail before dropping his head again and going back to sleep.

Pausing for a few seconds, Kyle straightened the tree, then placed the angel where she could continue watching over Meghan.

Then he started toward her. Kneeling beside the woman he intended to make his bride, he noticed the tracks that tears had traced down her face.

He'd caused her pain, he knew, and he had a lot to make up for.

Feathering her bangs back from her face, he murmured, "Merry Christmas, Meghan."

"Mmm." A smile flirted with her lips.

Softly, he kissed her earlobe, and his voice filtered through to her. "Meghan?"

Her eyes opened and she smiled even wider. "Nice dream." She closed her eyes again, then pulled her blanket—*their* blanket, he mentally amended—around herself.

Desperate times called for desperate measures, and Kyle

was a desperate man. He kissed her, seeking entrance to her mouth.

Her eyes opened abruptly and she struggled away, scooting back and sitting up. "Kyle!" She blinked several times, obviously not believing he actually stood there. "Did your motorcycle break down again?"

"The Beast is fine."

She pulled the blanket across her shoulders, as if trying to protect herself from further hurt. "Then, why...?"

The words had seemed so distant before, now they seemed real, and he knew he had to say them, wanted to say them. "Meghan, I love you."

She dragged her lip, the lower one, naturally, into her mouth. He wondered if she tasted him. Wondered what was going through her mind.

He reached for one of her hands, easing it away from its protective resting place near her heart.

"I was a fool not to recognize it earlier, a fool not to see how much you mean to me."

"But—"

"Say you'll marry me, be my wife."

He saw her swallow deeply. "I...I can't go to Chicago."

"I didn't ask you to."

She licked that slightly swollen lower lip. Her hesitation was still there, but she obviously wanted to believe.

"I'll stay here, with you." His heart thudded erratically, and he was losing his grip on the control he usually possessed.

"You said...what about the family business?"

"It doesn't matter." Drawing her hand to his lips, Kyle placed a kiss there. "You're all that matters."

"Oh, Kyle, I can't..." She trailed off, swallowed again. "I can't ask you to give up—"

"You asked for nothing, Meghan. Nothing. You took me in, gave me food and shelter, taught me about Christmas."

"No," she said, shaking her head. "You gave me the memories you promised. I'll have them forever."

"To go with the ones we'll make in the future."

She met his gaze, searching, imploring, almost begging him not to hurt her again. "You'd be giving up a fortune."

"I swear I'll spend the rest of my days trying to make you happy." Internally, his guts were constricted into painful knots. Nothing had ever mattered this much. No woman was Meghan. "Does it matter to you?"

"Money? Money doesn't matter to me, Kyle. Only love. I want children, want them to expect Santa, leave cookies out for him."

"As long as you leave me some milk to chase it down."

"Milk?" she repeated softly.

"A big glass."

A tear, shimmering in the light like diamond dust, pooled from her eye. He transferred the moisture onto his fingertip. He studied it, vowed this wonderful woman would never again cry over him. "From regret?" he asked softly, forcing the words around the tightness in his throat.

She shook her head.

"Then?" He held his breath.

"They're tears of happiness, Kyle, I'm so very happy."

"You'll...?"

"With my whole heart and soul, I love you. Yes, Kyle, yes. I'll marry you."

His breath rushed out in a single, ragged burst. The smile on her face was equal to a hundred sunrises, and it warmed his heart every bit as much.

He stood, pulling her with him. He gave her a gentle kiss, communicating his love, his commitment, his promise of happy memories from now on.

When she slowly ended the kiss, she traced her hands

down the sides of his face and whispered, "Merry Christmas, Kyle."

He glanced heavenward, thanking a holiday miracle for bringing them together. And he swore he heard the rustle of feathers from somewhere above....

Epilogue

"**A**nd a happy New Year!"

The notes of the out-of-tune carol faded, amid laughter and clapping. Meghan smiled, hugging her infant against her chest, feeling her heart swell with love.

The cold bite of a Colorado Christmas wind blasted the hayrack ride she was on, and she pulled a blanket higher over her.

"Who wants hot cider?" Kyle asked.

A chorus of voices responded enthusiastically. As her husband poured cider from a thermos into half a dozen cups, the cacophony of noise gradually faded.

He unwrapped plastic wrap from a plate and passed around cookies. "There's enough for three each," he said before moving through the hay to reach his wife's and baby's sides.

She scooted over to make room. Kyle draped his arm across her shoulder, peering down into the thoroughly adorable face of his daughter.

"You did good," he said, just like he had several times a day for the past months.

"*We* did good," she corrected him.

As the teenager they'd brought along led the underprivileged children into a discordant rendition of "Jingle Bells," Kyle held up a sprig of evergreen and stole a kiss from his wife.

"I suppose you want me to believe that's mistletoe?" she asked.

He shrugged.

"Kyle, I've told you, you don't need an excuse to kiss me."

"In that case..." He dropped the fake mistletoe.

"There are children around."

In the light of the lanterns that swung from the posts of the carriage bed, he looked up sheepishly, seeing inquisitive gazes focused on them. The teenager gave Kyle a thumbs-up.

"In that case, I'll collect later."

She shivered at the intensity of his gaze. "I'll hold you to that."

After another few songs, Kyle returned to the front of the wagon and reached for Aspen's reins. "Everyone ready?"

As the children, and Meghan, sang "Silent Night," he snapped the reins, heading toward the home they'd carved out...together.

Kyle now built cabinets for the numerous families who were constructing summer retreats in the South Park area, fulfilling his own dreams as well as earning enough money to keep his family comfortable. Sales of her angels had increased, and she now had full-time help, so she was free to fill the number of orders that were faxed in daily.

She looked up at Kyle. Obviously sensing her stare, he turned back to look at her. He smiled, and beneath the glow of a moon and the shimmering shine of heaven's Christmas stars, he mouthed ''I love you.''

Merrie, born exactly nine months after he'd returned to Meghan on Christmas Day, nuzzled her mother's breast. Meghan soothed a hand across her infant's head.

Christmas, she decided, was her favorite time of year. She felt complete. Her nights were silent no longer, and bad memories had been vanquished, replaced by good ones. Kyle continually gave her the greatest gift of all, love.

''But, Lexie, you watched Merrie last night,'' Grandma Aggie protested.

''Okay,'' said Lexie, reluctant to give up the honor of guarding the precious infant. ''Let's both stay with her. We'll keep her entertained while Meghan tells Kyle about their next miracle.''

''Their next miracle?'' Grandma Aggie said in awe. ''We'll have two to watch?''

Lexie nodded.

The tiny child shifted, stuffing fingers into her mouth. ''There's something special about this season,'' Lexie whispered.

From below, she heard the strains of a Christmas carol pouring from the cassette player. And, even though she shouldn't, she couldn't resist the impish impulse to part the atmosphere.

Kyle was unwrapping the present his wife had given him. He took in a breath, then allowed it to slowly release.

''Read the bottom,'' Meghan encouraged.

The angel was of a father, cradling a tiny infant. The father looked rather like Kyle, while the infant was obviously their baby.

On the bottom of the sculpture was an inscription, Merrie Christmas.

Kyle smiled, and as Meghan whispered her news, Lexie saw emotion sparkle in the corner of his eye.

Overcome herself, Lexie waved her wing, sealing the humans in their cocoon of love.

"And to all...a good night," she whispered, thinking that now, surely, Michael would find someone else to watch over that beastly little animal, Curiosity.

* * * * *

CHRISTINE FLYNN

Continues the twelve-book series—36 HOURS—in December 1997 with Book Six

FATHER AND CHILD REUNION

Eve Stuart was back, and Rio Redtree couldn't ignore the fact that her daughter bore his Native American features. So, Eve had broken his heart *and* kept him from his child! But this was no time for grudges, because his little girl and her mother, the woman he had never stopped—could never stop—loving, were in danger, and Rio would stop at nothing to protect *his* family.

For Rio and Eve and *all* the residents of Grand Springs, Colorado, the storm-induced blackout was just the beginning of 36 Hours that changed *everything!* You won't want to miss a single book.

Available at your favorite retail outlet.

**Help us celebrate
15 years of unforgettable
romance with**

▼ SILHOUETTE®

Desire®

You could win a genuine lead crystal vase, or
one of 4 sets of 4 crystal champagne flutes!
Every prize is made of hand-blown, hand-cut
crystal, with each process handled by master
craftsmen. We're making these fantastic gifts
available to be won by you, just for helping us
celebrate 15 years of the best romance reading
around!

DESIRE CRYSTAL SWEEPSTAKES
OFFICIAL ENTRY FORM

To enter, complete an Official Entry Form or 3" x 5"
card by hand printing the words "Desire Crystal
Sweepstakes," your name and address thereon and
mailing it to: in the U.S., Desire Crystal Sweepstakes,
P.O. Box 9076, Buffalo, NY 14269-9076; in Canada,
Desire Crystal Sweepstakes, P.O. Box 637, Fort Erie,
Ontario L2A 5X3. Limit: one entry per envelope, one
prize to an individual, family or organization. Entries
must be sent via first-class mail and be received no later
than 12/31/97. No responsibility is assumed for lost,
late, misdirected or nondelivered mail.

DESIRE CRYSTAL SWEEPSTAKES
OFFICIAL ENTRY FORM

Name: _____

Address: _____

City: _____

State/Prov.: _____ Zip/Postal Code: _____

KFO

15YRENTRY

Desire Crystal Sweepstakes
Official Rules—No Purchase Necessary

162

From the bestselling author of *Jury Duty*

Laura Van Wormer

It's New York City's most sought-after address—a prestigious boulevard resplendent with majestic mansions and impressive apartments. But hidden behind the beauty and perfection of this neighborhood, with its wealthy and famous residents, are the often destructive forces of lies and secrets, envy and undeniable temptations.

Step on to...

RIVERSIDE DRIVE

MIRA BOOKS

Available in January 1998–
where books are sold.

MLVW303

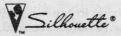